THE WEAKEST LINK

The Weakest Link

Cover Design: Nimra Bukhari
Published by "Independently Published"

DEDICATION

To my family, friends and readers: I am so thankful for the support and opportunity to keep writing, learning and entertaining all with my stories. Thank you for being patient, supportive and sharing your thoughts on my books.

CHAPTER 1

"Eligible Bachelor, Terrence J. Jenkins is now taken by a small town girl, Regina Ann Memphis, to be wed in Birch Creek" - This was the headline in the social column of the Chicago News Tribune. TJ and Reggie's photo was posted under the headline. It was taken at the green space dedication ceremony, when Reggie took her first trip to Chicago. As Reggie stared at the photo, she couldn't believe how much time had already passed since that day.

"TJ, come here and look!" Reggie was smiling at TJ as he entered the room.

"What is it?"

"Looks like I just won the prize, I got the most eligible bachelor in Chicago!" She reached over to kiss him.

"When did I become the most eligible bachelor?" he laughed.

"I bet all the Chicago socialites are wondering where the hell is Birch Creek?"

"They didn't print the date of the wedding did they?" TJ was concerned about the possibility of Rum Mason hearing about their wedding.

"No, it doesn't say. It mostly talks about you and your family and how much they are estimating you to be worth."

TJ rolled his eyes. Reggie smiled knowing how lucky she is to be marrying him. The thought had not crossed her mind about Rum finding out about their plans. As she stared at the article, her mind went back to the day she helped rescue Myra and Natalie. She will never forget the look in their eyes, the conditions all those girls were living in, how scared they all must have been. Three girls from her hometown, Birch Creek, were taken to be sold and trafficked by evil men who worked for Rumsfeld Mason, the most evil of them all! He had the largest human trafficking ring in the world but now it had been mostly destroyed. Reggie smiled as she remembered how all of the community in Birch Creek came together to help find Kendra, Myra and Natalie. TJ had brought in all the major news sources which helped the nation to be informed of what was going on in their small town. And then, the wonderful observant nurse in Savannah who realized Kendra was the unidentified patient he had lying in a coma in the ICU. Most of Rum's men had been arrested in connection with this world-wide trafficking network.

Several were arrested the day Reggie and the FBI found all the girls, including Myra and Natalie, at the compound in the Bahamas. Rum had not been found nor had the FBI been able to find any of his employees willing to give him up, actually, most didn't even know him. Rum had a calculating way of not being linked to any of it even though he was the one calling all the shots. He made everyone else do his dirty work.

"Reggie, did you hear what I said?" TJ asked.

"No, sorry, I was daydreaming about all that happened since the day that photo of us was taken. I want Rum caught and we have to figure out how to find him."

TJ sat next to her looking her in the eyes.

"Once he is caught, the FBI has to figure out how to link him to all of this. I know you have made it your mission to find him but don't let it take over your life. We have a wedding to plan and a wonderful life to live. Reggie, you did your job by finding the three missing girls from your hometown, mystery solved, remember?" He was serious about her being able to move on.

"I hear you and I love you. You ground me and protect me." She hugged him knowing that he meant well.

Right on cue, Sammy meowed and jumped up into her lap.

"And Sammy brings me back to reality. I'm going to take that as a sign. How did I get so lucky to be marrying you, have the best cat ever and be living on St. Simon's island in a magnificent house on the beach?"

"Reggie, you deserve everything in the world. Let me give it to you." TJ grabbed her hand kissing it.

CHAPTER 2

Rum Mason was still laying low somewhere in Europe. The exact location remained a mystery to everyone-everyone, that is, except his lover, Nick. For the last couple of weeks, Nick had been handling all the wedding plans for Reggie and TJ.

"Rum, I miss you so much! I hope I can see you soon."

"I miss you too."

It was too dangerous for them right now; any hint of their connection could expose them both. Rum had been a ghost for months, slipping through the hands of the FBI. Once a powerful figure who operated in the shadows, he was now the prime suspect in the largest human trafficking ring ever uncovered. He was the missing link and the FBI and Reggie still had no concrete evidence to tie him to this ring other than knowing exactly that he was the leader.

Federal agents had dismantled most of the network but Rum remained hidden. He had orchestrated everything from afar, leaving no direct evidence of his involvement. Even in hiding, Rum's need for control and revenge burned brighter than ever.

"Nick, call me after your meeting, we need to finalize their wedding reception finale." Rum laughed. His laugh was evil. He wanted to destroy any chance of Reggie finding him.

"Oh ok," Nick hesitated. He would do almost anything Rum asked of him but he didn't want to be in charge of hurting anyone.

"I've got to go. Talk later."

As Nick was ending the call, Reggie appeared in the doorway of the Birch Creek Chapel, the soft glow of the late afternoon light streaming through the stained glass windows. She was back in the town where it all began, at the place where she had always dreamed of saying her vows. Marrying TJ here would be her dream come true. As a young girl, when her parents were fighting and drinking causing chaos, she would run to this very chapel. She would sit on the creaky wooden pews. She would stare up at the kaleidoscope of colors cast by the windows and dream of her prince who would whisk her away to his castle. Now, standing here as a grown woman she was going to marry her prince soon. She took a deep breath letting the cool country air feel her lungs. She realized even though she had her prince, he hadn't rescued her; he had simply reminded her she had the courage to rescue herself.

"Hello Nick, I hope you didn't have any trouble finding this chapel way out here in the country." Reggie was walking towards the front of the church looking up at the beautiful wooden beams and the large stained glass windows. It all looked just as she remembered it.

"No, my GPS actually led me right to it. I assume this chapel has some sort of sentimental value to you? It looks like it hasn't been occupied in years."

Reggie ignored his question. She didn't want to share her reasons as to why she chose this chapel.

"TJ and I want the wedding to be intimate and very special with our family and friends sharing our day with us." Reggie sat down in the front pew as Nick was pulling out his plans.

"A Fall wedding is always so beautiful with cooler temperatures and the sun setting by six o'clock. When the wedding begins, the church will have a soft glow, lit up by candlelight.

Candles everywhere! No lights. The shimmering candles will be magnificent!" Nick showed Reggie a photo of the candles he was wanting to use.

"That looks beautiful. I want to caution you that we don't want to cause any sort of fire hazard."

"You let me handle all of that. Of course, I will make sure you approve everything." He smiled nervously knowing it wasn't going to be her dream wedding after all. Nick showed her all his ideas for the decor inside and outside of the chapel. Nick was careful not to show her the plans for the reception just yet. Reggie didn't know about the huge pavilion TJ was having built down by the river for the wedding reception. TJ had purchased the property as a wedding gift for Reggie. Nick wasn't going to bring up the reception for fear he would accidentally spoil the surprise.

"We decided on the caterer. It will be from TJ's favorite restaurant in Chicago. We still don't know yet where to have the reception, I'm going to check out a few places while I'm here in town."

"Oh ok, let me know as soon as you pick the place."

We aren't having a wedding cake because we want my friend Darlene to make all of her special pies. Nobody ever eats wedding cake anyway!"

Nick was thinking how tacky that sounded but wasn't going to tell Reggie. He would make it all elegant looking even if it was some hometown pies. He was getting to know Reggie and liked her so far. Her accent was special. He loved hearing her say, "Bless your heart."

"Where has the time gone?" Reggie was looking at her watch.

"Nick, I have to go meet someone. We can talk later about where to have the reception?" Nick was pulling out his tape measure.

"Yes, I'm just going to stay here for a few more minutes and take some measurements."

He wanted to walk down the path to the river to see the progress being made on the pavilion. He knew it was going to be beautiful.

"Ok, talk to you soon." Reggie left.

As soon as Reggie was out of sight, Nick walked down by the river to see the pavilion. There was no pavilion yet. The lot had been graded and concrete poured but that was all. The square footage had been marked off and flagged. River Birch trees lined the river making a shaded canopy over the water. Maybe he could put some lights in the trees to make it look more festive, he thought to himself. He really wanted it to look like an enchanted forest and be a dream wedding for Reggie. Rum does not need to be interfering with their wedding. What good will that do? It will only get him caught. He will convince Rum to leave it alone.

CHAPTER 3

Sheriff Johnson and his wife were sitting on their front porch drinking iced tea when Reggie arrived. They lived in a modest ranch style brick house which had been their home for at least the last 40 years. She was so excited to see them, it had been several months. They hugged her and she felt like she was their long lost daughter coming home.

Sheriff Johnson and his wife proceeded to walk inside. Reggie noticed Sheriff Johnson was limping and using a cane. He saw her looking at him.

"Yes, I have arthritis in my left hip. It acts up every now and then. Let's go inside and get you some iced tea. We can sit here." He motioned towards the living room. Reggie walked over towards the fireplace to get a closer look at all the recognitions and awards Sheriff Johnson had received over the years.

"All of these awards are so impressive." She glanced over at him.

"It's only because I've been around so long." He said in a soft low voice.

"Not true Sheriff, you earned every one of them."

Mrs. Johnson came in a few minutes later and handed her a tall glass of tea. As they sat down in the living room, Reggie wasted no time.

"Sheriff Johnson, I wanted to ask if you could walk me down the aisle on my wedding day?" HIs face lit up with a big smile. HIs wife grabbed his hand.

"I would be happy too. Maybe I won't have to use the cane." "Even if you do, it will be just fine."

"You will look so handsome walking a beautiful bride down the aisle." Mrs. Johnson beamed as she hugged him.

"Reggie, what about your father?" he asked.

"You know I wouldn't be able to rely on my father - he would either be drunk, not show up or not even remember that I asked him. Besides he hasn't been a father to me over all these years, my grandparents were more like my parents. At my grandfather's funeral, my parents didn't even know who I was."

"I'm so sorry you haven't been able to have much of a relationship with your parents," Sheriff Johnson looked at his wife.

"If truth be told, I am a hell of a lot better off not having a relationship with them. No more worry or heartache."

"I guess you're right."

"Well, that settles that!" Reggie knew she could count on him being there for her. I will send you all the details later about where to get fitted for your tuxedo."

"Tux? That sounds fancy."

"Not too fancy, remember it's a country wedding with a "city boy" groom. We need a little pizazz and class."

"Yes, I agree. I can handle it." Sheriff Johnson smirked.

"I told Darlene we would bring you to the restaurant when you arrived today. She has some pie waiting on you." He laughed, grabbing his keys motioning for them to follow him.

"Alright, that sounds wonderful. You can both help me decide which pies we want at the reception."

"Pies at the reception sounds like a Reggie wedding." Mrs. Johnson said as she reached over to hug her.

Reggie was so happy she had asked him to be the one to give her away. It would be perfect with him walking her down the aisle and Ed officiating the ceremony. Ed had officiated a couple of weddings a year or two earlier that she had attended. She remembered what a great ceremony they had turned out to be. Ed had kind of become the "wedding pastor" for all of the Sheriff's department employees.

CHAPTER 4

Rum was running out of employees to call on to carry out some of his work. Due to the FBI and Detective Reggie Memphis, the trafficking network was cut down to only a few groups in Japan. He still had some of "those bitches" under lock and key. The others were let go but he knew they couldn't tie him to any of it. Most of his employees had either disappeared or were in jail. He still had Domino under his thumb. Domino was loyal. He needed Domino to help carry out some of his Birch Creek project.

"Domino, have you seen the venue yet?" Rum was leaving a message from his new cell number. "Call me back."

Rum walked down to the cafe' down the street. No one there knew his real name. They called out to him everyday when he entered.

"Carlton, welcome."

Rum would nod to acknowledge the owner.

"I'll never be caught, no one here knows who I really am." Thinking to himself as he sat down at the table.

He knew Domino had to be loyal, he lost both of his best friends, Woody and Freddie, and had nothing else to lose. His cell phone vibrated.

"Hey, Domino, finally I hear from you. Have you looked at the venue?"

"Yes, I've seen it. Not much to see right now. The Pavilion isn't built yet. Only the concrete has been poured."

"I want the explosives to be put in the ceiling once it's built. Stay in touch." He hung up as the waiter came over to take his order.

As he ordered his usual, Minestrone Soup and grilled cheese sandwich, he heard a voice saying, "Make that 2." He looked up and was surprised to see Nick.

Rum stood embracing Nick as the waiter walked away.

"I caught the last flight out of Atlanta last night. I wanted to surprise you. I have some down time right now, so what better way to spend it." Nick smiled.

"I can't think of any better way either. This is a great surprise. Do you want some wine or champagne to celebrate?"

"Of Course."

After he ordered the champagne, he leaned in to whisper.

"What have you found out from Reggie about the investigation?"

"I haven't found out anything about the investigation. We don't discuss anything other than planning her wedding." Nick leaned back, not wanting to discuss anything about Reggie. He had not seen Rum in a few weeks and really was disappointed that Rum started right away discussing her but not surprised at all.

"Nick, I need you to find out if they have any more evidence. This is important to me. Not that I'm worried about myself because I'm not linked to any of it." He sipped the champagne.

"I talked to Domino who said he has looked at the venue and will be ready to install the explosives when the pavilion is built."

"Rum, you can't hurt people. All of those people could be badly hurt or die."

"I won't be the one doing it." He smirked.

"I need you to think about what you are planning and why? Why do you want to do this? It doesn't make sense other than you don't like Reggie. She was doing her job along with the FBI. You say they can't prove you are tied to any of it, so why do this now?"

"Reggie needs to pay for causing my network to collapse." Rum was clenching his jaw.

"Network? Collapsed? You still have Chinatech so I'm not sure what you mean."

"Don't play dumb with me, Nick. You know exactly what I'm talking about. You just choose to look the other way." Rum was confident that Nick knew about his network.

Nick just wanted to change the subject so he agreed to try to eavesdrop and try to find out more information.

"Rum, let's just enjoy the time I'm here with you. I have to leave again in a few days."

CHAPTER 5

Reggie stopped by the Sheriff's office before heading back to the airport. She wanted to see Ed and the rest of the team. Ed pulled her aside.

"Reggie, I'm so happy for you and TJ. I have something to tell you."

"Well, tell me already." Reggie knew Ed was excited which was rare for him to show this much emotion. He beamed with happiness.

"I have a girlfriend."

"What? Who? I'm so excited, tell me all about her."

"Darlene actually introduced us. She works at the salon where Darlene gets her hair cut. Her name is Marilyn and she is smart, beautiful and really nice."

"Well, it doesn't surprise me at all that Darlene played matchmaker. I can't wait to meet her. You have to bring her to the wedding. Ed, you are actually blushing. It must be love."

"Well, she is great but we are still just getting to know each other." He then pulled out a photo of the 2 of them at a local restaurant.

"She looks beautiful and you look so happy too."

"I am happy Reggie." Ed put the photo back in his top left jacket pocket. It was as if he carries it around in his jacket pocket every day.

That is so sweet and it made her wonder if TJ carries around a photo of her and him. "Can we talk business for a minute?" Reggie asked.

"I thought you would never ask. The FBI has had an informant report that Rum is in Rome. Italy."

Reggie was trying to picture where Rum would be hiding in Rome.

"Do they think this informant knows what he is talking about? Have they seen him?"

"I don't know the details. They have sent some agents to check it out. So this person must be reliable."

"That is fantastic news. Keep me updated. What if he was found and arrested before our wedding? That would be an even greater celebration. He needs to be caught and in prison soon. I can't believe all the criminal acts he has committed. It's way too many but you better believe we will count all of them and charge him for every last one when he is caught. He has ruined so many lives." Reggie could feel the heat rising up her chest and neck.

"Reggie, I will let you know when I hear anything. He will be caught one day. He will make a big mistake and get caught, I am sure of that. I can't imagine how many women have been abused by the hands of such a narcisstic evil man." Reggie hugged him and then walked towards the door.

"You are always positive and I love that about you, Ed. I will send all the wedding details, rehearsal times, dinner and tuxedo information.

"Tuxedo?"

"Yes, that is exactly what Sheriff Johnson questioned too. I will tell you like I told him. It's a small town country wedding with a "City Boy" groom. We need to glam it up some!"

"Alright, I hear you! Maybe my bow tie can have some sequins or something!" Reggie laughed knowing Ed would rather die than wear a sequined bow tie.

"I have to head to the airport now but take care of Marilyn and Sheriff Johnson. I noticed his limp and cane."

"Yes, he is slowing down but still doesn't want to retire. He gets around just fine but some days his hip acts up more than other days. He walks every morning.

Marilyn's going to love you, I can't wait to introduce you to her next time you are in town."

CHAPTER 6

Reggie was still adjusting to the surreal experience of being chauffeured to the airport to board a private jet. She wasn't the type to crave luxury or demand special treatment; her practical, grounded nature resisted the indulgence. Yet, here she was stepping into a world that felt both exciting and foreign. During the ride to the airport, She was imagining Rum being caught in Rome and the news of it being blasted all over the major networks. She quickly came back to reality, a luxurious, wonderful reality when she boarded the plane. The flight back to St. Simon's Island was brief, giving Reggie just enough time to focus on the wedding guest list. As she reviewed the names, a thought struck her-she hadn't asked Nick if he planned to bring a guest. The idea nagged at her. Nick had poured so much of himself into the wedding plans, and the last thing she wanted was for him to feel like just the help on her special day. She was getting to know him and she knew he deserved to relax and enjoy it too, even if just for a moment. She would ask him the next time they talked. When the jet landed, TJ was waiting for her. He ran up the steps as usual to hug her and help her disembark. TJ grabbed her hand as they got seated in the limo.

"Reggie, I have some great news."

"Tell me."

"Reggie, my parents are coming to visit. They want to spend some time with us and get to know you better. My mother is so excited to hear about the wedding plans."

"That will be wonderful, when are they coming?"

"They are arriving this afternoon."

"OMG, this afternoon, I need to clean and get things ready. Hurry up and let's get home." Reggie was making a list in her head of everything she needed to do before they arrive, "It's all taken care of, baby. I want you to relax and enjoy their visit."

Reggie was surprised when they arrived at home, he did think of everything. The refrigerator and pantry were stocked. The house was clean including all the laundry done and sheets changed with fresh towels in the bathroom.

"You are the prince that I dreamed of as a child. I love you." Reggie shouted to TJ who was in the living room. TJ was working on his latest novel. He was doing research about sunken ships in the area, while waiting for his parents to arrive.

Reggie sat down on her bed. She wants everything to be perfect for her soon to be in-laws. She wasn't sure how to be a daughter-in-law. She heard Sammy meow about the time he jumped in her lap.

"Sammy, how do you know the exact time that I need your reassurance?" She laughed and petted Sammy. HIs purring is always calming to her.

TJ's parents arrived with several suitcases in tow. Reggie hadn't asked how long they were staying but it looked like a week or two judging the size and amount of luggage. After all the greetings were done, TJ immediately wanted to show his father the "low country boil" he was preparing for their dinner. He had learned to cook many seafood dishes while living on the coast. TJ loved being able to cook out on the deck looking out at the ocean view. He loved buying fresh seafood everyday and cooking for the two of them. Now, he would get to show off his new cooking talent to his parents.

Reggie was showing his mother around the house when Mrs. Jenkins grabbed her hand.

"Regina, I have a gift for you. I hope you will like it. I thought you might wear it on your wedding day."

As they walked into the guest room, she unzipped her luggage and pulled out a beautiful box handing it to Reggie. It was a beautiful pearl bracelet.

"This is so beautiful and perfect for me to wear with my dress. Thank you so much." Reggie knew it was a lovely gesture for his mother to show she was welcoming her as her daughter-in-law.

"I've never seen my son so happy. He truly loves you and I can tell you feel the same."

"TJ is the best person I've ever met. I love him so much. TJ and I are so excited to have you come here and see our home."

TJ prepared and cooked his low country boil to perfection. The four of them ate out on the back deck with the ocean as the backdrop to a perfect setting. The sun had already set with a bright full moon rising. As the plates were cleared, TJ suggested they go for a walk.

"That's a great idea. The moon is bright enough we may not even need flashlights." Reggie said as she handed a silk wrap to TJ's mother.

"Take this wrap, the wind gets chilly."

As they walked along the shore with their bare feet sinking in the sand, Mr. Jenkins stopped staring out at the ocean.

"You know there is something about the ocean, it reminds you how life just keeps moving, whether you're paying attention or not."

"That's deep dad. Are you getting philosophical with us?"

"It's easy to let time slip by sometimes without focusing on what really matters. I would like to make a request."

"Go on," TJ was intrigued.

"After the wedding, I think we should start a family tradition to include all of us, your sisters and their families too. It will be something to keep us connected no matter what life throws at us."

"What kind of tradition?" Reggie asked.

"A yearly family vacation. No distractions, no work, just us. A chance for us to be together making family memories."

"I bet each year, the family grows too." TJ's mother shouted. "We need some little ones running around."

"I've never been on a family vacation before." Reggie spoke softly.

Mr. Jenkins grabbed Reggie's hand and turned to her.

"Well, it's time to change that. Starting next year, we'll pick the spot, pack our bags and make it happen. You're part of the family now, Reggie, and family means taking time for each other."

"I like that, count me in."

TJ hadn't realized that Reggie had never been on a family vacation before. He took that sort of thing for granted. He grabbed her hand, pulling her close.

They smiled and continued walking along the edge of the shore. The moment felt easy and full of promise, the perfect beginning to a new family tradition. Reggie couldn't believe how lucky she was.

During the week,they spent time together walking along the beach, eating great seafood and shopping. Mrs. Jenkins wanted to buy wedding gifts for them but they already had everything they ever needed. Reggie had declined on the idea of having any wedding showers. She just wanted to focus on their wedding and spending the rest of her life with TJ. Reggie was feeling more confident about her relationship with Mr. and Mrs. Jenkins after spending some time with them.

A week had passed quickly and it was time for TJ's parents to go back to Chicago. They would be seeing them again in a few weeks for the wedding. As they were cleaning up their breakfast dishes, TJ poured each of them another cup of coffee.

"There is something I want to tell you, Reggie. I have a surprise. It's my wedding gift to you." He had that nervous smile showing his dimples on one side.

"You're being mysterious, out with it." Reggie sat up straighter in her chair.

TJ took a deep breath.

"I bought the land by the Birch Creek Chapel down by the creek."

Reggie looked at his parents and then back at him, not sure if she heard him correctly.

"What, you bought it?"

He nodded.

"Yes, it's ours now. And I'm having a pavilion built there. It will be ready just in time for our reception."

Reggie was speechless.

"That's a beautiful idea." His mother stood up clapping her hands.

"Reggie, Nick already knows about the pavilion. He has been helping me plan the reception around it. I wanted it to be perfect for you."

Reggie jumped up and hugged TJ.

"Nick knew and didn't say anything?" She asked.

"I swore him to secrecy. He has some amazing ideas for making the space look incredible for the reception."

"I can't wait to see it and see Nick's ideas." TJ held up his hand.

"Wait there's more. After the wedding, I was thinking we should donate the land to the town. Turn it into a park where families can picnic and play by the creek. It will be a place that brings families together."

"I love that idea. You think of everything, TJ. You are incredible and I don't know how to thank you." Reggie hugged him again.

TJ's mother sighed. "It's going to be a beautiful wedding. I bet more couples will want to use that chapel and the pavilion. They can use it for birthday parties and family reunions too. What an incredible way to give back to the community."

CHAPTER 7

Nick was packing his clothes getting ready to head back to the airport, when Rum came in. Nick had realized since being gone for a few weeks and then returning to see Rum that he was having some different feelings. He wasn't as dependent on Rum as he thought. It had been good to spend time away.

"Nick, I really need you to find out what Reggie and the FBI are doing and what they know. I also need you to understand that on the day of the wedding, you will be the one to trigger the explosives." Nick turned quickly around to face Rum.

"I can't be a part of hurting anyone. I will not do it. A lot of people could die." Nick had never stood up to Rum.

Rum moved in closer.

"You will do it, you have to." Rum stared at Nick. His veins in his neck were bulging.

"You think this will distract the feds from looking for you, this will make them come after you even more." Nick yelled and could feel himself shaking.

"No, it will seem as if the builders did a faulty job in the wiring. They will never suspect me."

Nick continued to pack his clothes. He wanted to leave as soon as possible.

"Nick, you promised me. You said you'd stand by me. All I need is a little cooperation. You know what's at stake here."

"I didn't sign up for this. You're going too far. You have lost your mind."

"If you think you can walk out of here and betray me, think again." Rum moves in closer to Nick. Rum moved as close to him as possible without touching him.

"You are either with me or against me."

Nick took a few steps back and grabbed his luggage. With a trembling voice, "Then I'm against you."

Nick turned to walk out, not looking back, afraid to look.

"Then don't ever come back." Rum was red-faced and yelling as Nick shut the door.

Rum sat down at the window thinking about what to do next. He knew he had to move quickly. Who does Nick think he is? He wants to go against me after all I have done for him. He better not tell Detective Memphis nor anyone else how to find me. He had to plan quickly.

He would go to Africa next to escape, that's it, Africa. He would come up with a different plan to destroy the wedding and distract Reggie and the FBI. Nick had to pay for his disobedience.

Rum called Domino.

"Change of plans. We won't do the explosives after all. There needs to be another kidnapping. Kidnap someone close to Reggie. I need you to come up with the details. Let me know once you've decided who, how, when and where. Then I'll give you further directions."

"Yes, sir." Domino agreed and didn't ask any questions. Domino learned not to question but do exactly as Rum ordered.

CHAPTER 8

Nick returned to the states knowing he had to make it on his own. He changed his flight to New York instead of Georgia. He had to come up with a plan for himself. He knew Rum would never let him come back, nor did he want to. Rum would think of him as untrustworthy since he didn't carry out his demands. He was terrified to live on his own but felt the weight off his shoulders. He didn't want all of Rum's dealings on his conscience anymore even though he wasn't exactly sure what those dealings were. He had overheard conversations that he wanted to forget. He was not going to be implicated in any of it. He would keep his mouth shut and go about his own business.

When his flight landed in New York, he checked his phone. Three missed calls from *"Rum Lover"*. He would not return his calls.

Nick decided he would call his best friend from school, Betty. Betty would help him get back on his feet. Nick grew up in a small town in New York. He was a dreamer. A kid who loved art, design and imagining a life far away from the trailer park where he grew up with his mother, His mother worked long hours and his father left when he was too young to remember him. When he was in his early twenties, he moved to Manhattan, hoping to break into the event planning business. He had a natural talent for creating magical spaces and coordinating the perfect parties and weddings. His creativity and charm attracted wealthy clients and that is how he reconnected with Betty, a friend since middle school. Betty had married well into a family of bankers. Years ago, Rum met Nick at a party that Betty had hired Nick to plan. Later, Rum hired him to plan an extravagant private party. When the event was a huge success, Rum promised Nick endless opportunities, connections and resources.

As Nick grew closer to Rum, he began to suspect that Rum's wealth and influence came from darker places. His requests for secrecy and last-minute changes and cash only transactions raised some red flags with Nick. Nick decided it wasn't any of his business what type of business dealings Rum was doing. Rum had given his career the boost it needed.

Over time, as lovers, Nick felt trapped and weak. But now, Nick may have reached his breaking point. He had actually stood up to Rum.

Betty was so excited to hear from Nick.

"Nick, how long has it been since I last saw you? You have to come over today."

"Well, that's my intention to come and see you and ask a favor." He agreed to go to her house right away.

Betty's house was even more spacious and beautiful than he remembered. It was a tudor style with 4 large bedrooms that overlooked a courtyard and pool. As he peered out the large french doors, he noticed another building just off the pool area.

"Betty, have you added on since I was here last?"

"Yes, that is my craft room out back. I have been creating all kinds of things. Flower arrangements, wreaths, and also started sewing again. I have made tablecloths, placements, napkins and table runners.

"You must show me. I can use your creativity in my event planning."

They looked at her new craft room and all the things she had made. Time had passed since they had last talked but they picked up as though they were still best friends from middle school.

Betty made all the arrangements for Nick to stay in one of their rental apartments. He couldn't believe how beautiful and spacious it was for a New York apartment.

"Betty, you are an angel. I wasn't sure where I could afford to live. Now, you have changed that for me. This is what I needed after my break up."

Betty knew Nick had a partner but didn't know anything about him. She didn't pry and Nick was relieved. He was going to be ok without Rum.

CHAPTER 9

Domino had spent the past few weeks on the move, slipping in and out of Birch Creek, Chicago and St. Simon's like a shadow. His task was clear, but the execution required precision. Timing was everything, when to strike, how to execute the plan, and most importantly, who to target. Every detail had to be perfect, every step calculated. As he trailed Reggie and TJ, watching from a distance, he studied their routines. He knew Rum's plan had to be carried out with no trace of evidence leading back to Rum, the mastermind.

Domino had painstakingly studied TJ and Reggie's monotonous routine over the past couple of weeks. Morning jogs along the beach, evenings spent at home and predictable trips into town. It was almost too dull to watch. But then the pattern broke, TJ's parents had arrived for a visit. At first, Domino saw an opportunity. TJ's mother seemed like an easy target, kind, trusting and distracted by the wedding plans but it didn't take long to realize that she was never alone. She was always surrounded by either her husband or her son and future daughter-in-law.

Domino became frustrated but undeterred. He had another option in mind. Sheriff Johnson was a possible target. Domino would change his course of action and travel back to Birch Creek.

As he trailed Sheriff Johnson for a couple of days, he became more convinced that the sheriff was the right target. He was rugged, authoritative and respected in the community. And he had ties to Reggie that made him valuable. Unlike TJ's mother, the sheriff's independence made him vulnerable.

Domino had his target, now he needed to figure out his next steps to execute a plan.

Domino carefully monitored the sheriff's schedule noting when he is most isolated. The sheriff walks every morning from the office to the post office to check their post office box. The post office doesn't open to the public until nine so usually he is alone checking the mail. There aren't any traffic lights between the sheriff's office and the post office, less cars to worry about. Also, he observed that the sheriff rarely has his gun on him during his morning walk. This walk is routine for him so he won't be on high alert. He knows the kidnapping has to be quick and efficient. He will park the van along the sheriff's route and wait until sheriff Johnson is out of sight of anyone. He will wear a uniform to blend in as a maintenance worker or utility crew member. The plan is set. He called Rum. No answer.

"Rum, I have my target and next steps ready, just give me the go ahead." He left a voicemail message hoping to hear back quickly from him. He had no idea where Rum was even hiding out at this point. It could be in the middle of the night wherever he is.

Domino would go to his own hideout in Savannah to get it ready and wait on further instructions. He would have to wait until a weekday when he knew the sheriff would be on duty. Domino was rarely able to go to his Savannah location due to always doing surveillance or carrying out Rum's orders.

Domino's hideout was a home in Savannah on the marsh. He had views of the Savannah river where the marsh spilled into it. The marsh was filled with wildlife that he experienced every time he was there whether it was fishing, crabbing or just looking out at the sunset. The marsh was his home. His airboat had come in handy many times in those shallow waters. He would bring the sheriff here and put up any personal items so as to not give away that it was his home. Domino had never married nor had a love interest. He used women and then left them, he didn't have time for relationships.

Domino's phone rang. *"Unknown caller."*

"Hello?"

"You called me earlier." Rum's voice was cold, direct.

"Yes, everything's in place, boss. The target will be Sheriff Johnson. His routine hasn't changed. I will grab him on a weekday morning whenever you give the go-ahead. It will be quick and I will take him to a remote place and wait for your next instructions."

"Good. Clean and quick. No mistakes, Domino. You know what happens when there are mistakes." Rum swirls his glass of wine before taking a sip.

Domino hesitated.

"Yeah, I know, no loose ends." "Take him on Monday."

"Yes, sir. I will call you when the target is secured."

Rum ends the call, tossing the phone onto the desk and walking out on his balcony. Despite being in another country, he feels as though he is in complete control, with one exception-Nick. What to do about Nick. He called Nick's cell phone again. No answer. This time he texted him a message knowing Nick would know it was him even if from a different cell number.

"Call me. Consequences for your actions are reality."

Rum had some resources from the past that he could count on. These resources always fall for his blackmail threats. He called Jerry, a former employee and tech genius.

"Jerry, I need you to find Nick. I want to know where he is living. I know he is working, planning a wedding in Birch Creek but he wouldn't dare live there. Find out everything you can." Rum knew Jerry could find out within minutes all of Nick's recent moves. Jerry had worked for Rum but left his company when he realized what was really going on. Rum had him intertwined with it all without him realizing until it was too late. They made an agreement that he could quit with strings attached-he would need to help him out whenever he called on him.

"Find him? Is he not living with you anymore? How recent is this?" Jerry knew when he answered the 'unknown caller' that it would be Rum.

"It's recent, within the last couple of weeks. He is probably staying with someone, he is nothing without me. He can't afford to buy a place. Call me back at this number." Rum hung up the phone.

Jerry called back within the hour after scanning all his resources. He knew Rum was up to something, Nick must have stood up to him and left. He wanted to give Rum the information and be done. He didn't want to know about anything that was happening.

"Rum, Nick flew to New York. He is staying in an apartment in Manhattan, owned by a banking firm.

"Send me the information for the apartment and the banking firm, ASAP." Rum ended the call. He was angry and wondering how Nick was able to have an apartment in Manhattan. Did he have a new lover?

Rum received the information and called Domino without hesitation.

"Domino, you are going to New York. I have Nick's new address. I need you to find out how he is affording a Manhattan apartment and who he might be living with. Scare him enough so he won't tell what he knows. Go to New York then we will worry about the sheriff."

"Alright, boss. Send me the information and I will leave right away." Domino was already packing his things to leave on a moment's notice which he was used to doing now.

CHAPTER 10

Reggie couldn't wait to talk with Nick. She called him to arrange their next meeting.

"Nick, TJ shared his surprise wedding gift with me and you knew about it all along."

"Yes, I was so afraid I was going to accidentally say something about it. I'm glad you know about it now so we can finalize some details."

"Can we meet tomorrow either here at my house or in Birch Creek? You know, I was thinking, I don't even know where you live. I also wanted to tell you that you can bring a guest with you to the wedding. I want you to enjoy our special day."

Nick hesitated for a minute before speaking. He wasn't sure how to respond.

"Yes, I can come to Birch Creek so we can discuss the reception details. I just recently moved to Manhattan. My partner and I recently broke up. I wouldn't want to bring a guest anyway because I will be working. It's fun for me to see how it all comes together."

"Is tomorrow ok since you are coming all the way from Manhattan? Let me send our jet to pick you up."

"Well, that would be fantastic, if you can send it." Nick was thankful for her nice gesture.

"Of course, I will text you all the details, where to meet at the airport to board the jet."

Reggie and TJ decided to drive to Birch Creek because they sent the pilot to Manhattan to pick up Nick. Reggie wanted to get there earlier so they could see the progress on the pavilion and walk along the creek.

"TJ, I still can't believe you bought this property. It is such a lovely setting for our reception and will make a great park for the public. Look at how much those River Birch trees have grown since I last saw the creek. I think we should build some walkways and maybe a bridge or two so everyone can explore the other side of the creek."

"We can do all of that. Should we think of a name for the park?" TJ asked. "Hmmm, I need to think about that."

Reggie wanted to show TJ the most special spot along the river.

"Ok, stop, close your eyes and turn around." She said TJ followed her commands.

"Can I open my eyes now?"

"Yes, look at this view."

TJ was looking up at the view of the mountains and the rushing waters of the creek flowing beside them.

"This is spectacular, Reggie." She grabbed his hand.

"Wait until you see the sun setting and shining on the mountains. Growing up with this view, made me realize the significance of the words "Purple Mountains Majesty" in the song, "America." You can't imagine what that means until you actually see the purple mountains."

"That's it Reggie, 'Purple Mountains Majesty' park.

"Yes, that would be perfect. We can put some benches in this area for everyone to sit and watch the mountains turn purple as the sun shines on them. I love it."

As they arrived at the pavilion, the building crew was there installing all the huge wooden posts. The walkway leading up to the pavilion was large flat rock pavers that flowed into the rock floors of the pavilion.

"Reggie, how about we have an amphitheater built along this side of the pavilion?" TJ said as he pointed to the left side.

"I love that idea, it could be used for so many things. Yes, let's do it."

As TJ was describing plans with the builder, Nick arrived. Reggie saw him walking down the path leading to the pavilion.

"Nick, I'm so glad you were able to come on such short notice. Was your flight ok?"

"It was an easy, wonderful flight."

Reggie pointed at the folding chairs and table the builders brought for the workmen. "Let's sit here and look at your plans for the reception area."

Nick opened his large tote bag and pulled out several folders. He showed the flower arrangements he picked out along with the candles and ice sculptures. The sketches he drew of how it was all going to be arranged was the last folder he pulled out.

"These are beautiful. You have done a magnificent job. I would like for you to pick out some permanent garden sculptures to be installed permanently."

"Of course, I can do that. Tell me what you have in mind."

The builder came over to talk with Nick about the plans. As they were talking, Reggie noticed Nick's cell phone vibrating on the table. She read: *"Rum Lover" calling.*

Her heart started beating faster. "Rum lover?" she said to herself. She wasn't sure what it meant, but the familiarity of the name made her stomach tighten. Could it be a coincidence? Is it Rum or just someone who likes to drink Rum? She motioned for TJ. He was busy talking with the workmen. Should she ask Nick?

Reggie hesitated. She could confront him now, demand answers, but something inside her told her not to. She didn't want to start a confrontation-not just yet. At that moment, Nick looked at his phone, rolling his eyes. She watched him carefully put his phone in his pocket. He didn't realize that she saw who was calling. Her pulse quickened as her mind raced. Rum? Was it him? Why was he calling Nick? What was the connection between them?

Now, she couldn't think of anything else. If it's Rum, she would bide her time. The more she could learn, the better. Nick could be the key. He might be the weakest link in this twisted puzzle. He could lead her to Rum.

" Reggie, did you hear me? Are you ok? You seem distracted." Nick asked.

"Sorry, I was just thinking of something I forgot to do. My schedule is busy these days." She realized she needed to remain calm.

TJ walked over and noticed she was twirling her finger in her hair. He knew she was anxious about something.

"Hey Reggie, take a walk with me so we can discuss the park plans." He motioned to her to come on. As they walked up the trail to the chapel, TJ was thinking Reggie was getting anxious about the wedding.

"Reggie, it's all going to be beautiful and work out just fine."

"It's not that, I have to tell you what I think I saw." She stopped and looked at TJ. "What is it, I can tell something is bothering you?"

"Nick's phone was laying on the table when he was talking to the builder. He was getting a phone call and when I glanced at this phone, it said 'Rum Lover' calling.

"Are you sure that's what it said?"

"Yes, and when he finally looked at his phone, he rolled his eyes and put it in his pocket." TJ sat down on the steps outside of the chapel. He was looking at his phone.

"That son of a bitch, that's why we recognized him. He was the one in some of the photos that we looked at on Rum's social media. Now, I can't find him. Rum has deleted all of his accounts."

Reggie sat down beside TJ while he scrolled through his phone. She closed her eyes, her mind was racing.

"This changes everything. Have we been set up? Is Rum lover, Rumsfeld Mason? Nick told me he recently broke up with his partner. We can't confront him, we need to find out more." Reggie's stomach churned.

TJ rubbed his temples, his head was hurting. He was getting so angry thinking about the connection.

"Nick has been around us for weeks, planning the wedding. If he is connected to Rum, it's like we are handing him everything on a silver platter-the venue, the guest list, the timeline. You and I know Rum was the one behind your house exploding, we just don't have the proof yet.

Reggie, I'm thinking we need some secret security detail. We don't know what all Rum is capable of or what he may be planning."

As they sat on the front steps of chapel, they saw Nick walking down the path towards them.

"Don't say anything, Reggie. We can use this as an opportunity." TJ smiled.

Nick had his bag with him looking as though he was getting ready to leave.

"I'm finished for now. I will go home and work on these plans and get back to you as soon as I can. Time is getting away from us, the wedding is soon and adding new items is getting me anxious but you know I will handle it." Nick said as he loaded up his bag in the rental car.

"Our pilot will fly you back to New York whenever you are ready." TJ said as he grabbed Reggie's hand gripping it tightly.

"Again, thank you both so much. I certainly appreciate your hospitality. This wedding is going to be fabulous!"

They waved goodbye, not knowing what was being planned by these criminals.

"We need to go meet with Ed and tell him everything. He will be able to look up all of Rum's social media even if it has been shut down. We need to confirm that it is Nick in those photos we remember seeing."

"Well, let's go. I want to get both of those sons of bitches. I can't believe we have been tricked by Nick. What in the hell do you think they are planning?"

Nick called Ed to let him know they needed to meet him right away. TJ was going to arrange some security details as soon as they confirmed it was Nick.

After they explained what had happened, their suspicions were confirmed. Ed was able to look up the information and found the photos they had previously seen.

"It is Nick." TJ slammed his fist on the table.

"I can't believe this is happening. Are we in danger?" Reggie asked.

"Yes, you are. Your house was blown up, remember? We have to notify the sheriff and the FBI. We need a plan in place." Ed's face was red.

They met with the Sheriff and called the FBI agent. The FBI would put together all the information they could gather on Nick which should include Rum. Nick was going to be back in New York until a week before the wedding. The FBI insisted on having some agents from their team to be the security detail for TJ and Reggie.

"Reggie, had you not seen his cell phone, we wouldn't know any of this and there is no telling what could have happened. Nick doesn't realize he is the weakest link!" TJ's voice was raised from being anxious.

"It will take a couple of days to devise a plan to trap Nick in his lies and lead us to Rum." Sheriff Johnson replied.

"Everyone needs to be careful and on alert." Ed said.

CHAPTER 11

Domino travels to Manhattan. He finds the apartment building where Nick is staying very quickly. It's in the heart of Manhattan, a large complex with marble siding. He watched the residents coming and going all day. No sign of Nick yet. He knew Nick was living on the 12th floor. He didn't want to act just yet. He had to make sure Nick was home when he entered his apartment. He would have to get past the doorman too. As Domino sat on a nearby bench watching for Nick, he saw two men approach the doorman. They are dressed in black suits, crew cuts and looking like the Feds. He saw one pull out a photo to show to the doorman. The doorman nodded, yes. The FBI has to be on to Nick, he couldn't take a chance on getting caught by them. They might have others surveying the scene as he sits waiting. Domino looked around slowly observing everyone around him. He stands and walks into a nearby coffee shop. He texted Rum.

"I'm here at Nick's apartment building. The FBI is on the scene asking the doorman questions. I have to see how this plays out before I strike."

Rum responds: *"Nick must have revealed some information."*

"No, I think they are looking for him, asking questions." Domino answered.

"Get out of there. Go on to Birch Creek and carry out the plan."

Rum sat at his desk, tapping his fingers on the arm of the chair. He closed the curtains. He was feeling like they had to be getting closer to making more arrests but it wasn't going to be him. They will not catch me. If they interview Nick, what's going to happen? Nick will be scared, he will cooperate if pushed. No one, not even Nick knew his whereabouts this time.

Domino arrived back in Birch Creek late on Sunday night. It had been a couple of days since he talked to Rum. He planned to go ahead with the plan as soon as possible. He needed sleep before the attack. He slept in his van until early the next morning. He was prepared.

It was a quiet morning with the exception of faint sounds of dogs barking. Domino has already seen the Sheriff's car parked at the office earlier. Domino had carefully searched for any nearby cameras and parked the van so it wasn't in any camera views. He needed to grab the sheriff on his way to the post office. Just as expected, Domino spotted Sheriff Johnson walking his usual route with his cane and not wearing his holster. Domino was dressed in a utility worker's uniform and wearing a hat, gloves and sunglasses. He had the cloth with chloroform on it in his back pocket. He left the side door of the van slightly open. All of a sudden, the Sheriff stopped and turned to look behind him. He stood still for a few seconds then kept walking. Domino thought he might have heard him opening the van door behind the fenced in area. As the Sheriff got close enough, Domino grabbed him from behind, holding the cloth up to his mouth and nose. He was quickly falling to the ground. Domino quickly pulled him behind the fence and loaded him into the van. He ran back checking for anyone or cars and grabbed his cane that he dropped on the sidewalk. He covered up the Sheriff with a blanket and knew he would be out for a while. He put zip ties around his feet and hands and put duct tape over his mouth. He tied a blind fold to cover his eyes. He took his phone and would throw it out along the highway once they got out of town. Domino's movements were precise, he stayed calm. This wasn't his first job, nor would it be his last. The quiet street remained unchanged, no evidence of any criminal activity taking place. As he drove through town, he was thinking that was way too easy. He's the sheriff and that was easier than kidnapping some of the girls. It would probably be hours before anyone even realized he was missing. By the time it was discovered, they would be close to Savannah.

CHAPTER 12

Mrs. Johnson had prepared their lunch as usual, she was wiping her hands on a dish towel looking up at the clock. It was almost 12, time for lunch. Her husband kept the same routine unless he was called to a crime scene which rarely happened. At 12:15, she called his phone. No answer. She was thinking he probably got held up at work. She would go ahead and eat her lunch and warm up his plate if he didn't show up soon. She ate her lunch and looked at the clock again, 12:45. Surely, he would call her if he wasn't able to come home for lunch. She called his cell phone again, this time leaving a message.

"Hey it's me, let me know if you can't make it home in time for lunch. I can save it for later if needed. Call me."

She hung up feeling uneasy, he always answered her calls. By 2:00 PM, she was worried and called the office, pacing in her kitchen. She asked to speak to Ed.

"Ed, have you seen my husband? He didn't come home for lunch and he isn't answering his cell phone." Her voice was shaking.

"No, I haven't seen him all day, I thought he was taking the day off. He hasn't been here since I arrived. Let me look in his office to see if he has a meeting in town marked on his calendar. I will call you back."

Ed walked into the Sheriff's office and immediately knew he had been in his office earlier. He had some coffee left in his cup sitting on his desk and the coffee maker was on. His gun and holster were laying in his chair. Ed ran up to the front desk area, knowing something was wrong.

"Have any of you seen the Sheriff this morning? His wife says he didn't come home for lunch. I thought he was off today." Ed yelled.

No one had seen him. His car was in the parking lot, someone shouted.

"Has anyone seen the mail, did he go pick it up?" Ed asked.

No mail. Several started calling his cell phone, it went straight to voicemail. One deputy said he would walk down to the post office to check the mail and see if they saw him.

Ed calls Mrs. Johnson back.

"No one has seen him today. His car is here along with his gun and holster." The silence on the other end of the phone was deafening.

"We will be looking for him and I will call you back." Ed knew this wasn't like him and knew something had happened.

By late afternoon, the word had spread in town that no one could find the sheriff. Deputies were searching all around town. By that evening, everyone was on edge. One deputy was at the Johnson home with his wife. Ed called Reggie knowing she was back home in St. Simon's.

"Reggie, the sheriff is missing." Ed's voice sounded tired. "Missing? What do you mean, I don't understand."

"He didn't go home for lunch, so his wife called me. None of us have seen him today. His gun and holster were on his desk and his car was in the parking lot."

"TJ and I will be on our way. Call me if you find anything." Reggie hung up telling TJ what Ed told her.

"Reggie, it sounds like he has been taken. I can't help but think this is the work of Rum." "Oh please don't let that be the case." Reggie sighed.

When Reggie and TJ arrived in Birch Creek, it was in the early morning hours. They went straight over to the Johnson home. The outside and inside lights were all on, several cars were in the driveway. Friends had come over to stay with his wife. Reggie walked in and hugged her and held her hand. Mrs. Johnson's expression was grim.

As the search intensified in Birch Creek, Domino had reached his Savannah hideout. The Sheriff was awake but Domino wasn't speaking to him. Domino had covered the Sheriff's eyes with a bandana so he couldn't identify him. They were several hours south of Birch Creek in the outskirts of Savannah. Domino leaned against the doorway, smoking a cigarette, listening to the sound of the frogs and wildlife in the marsh. He had called and texted Rum to let him know the job was done. He made the sheriff lay down on a bed and handcuffed him to the bed. Domino knew they wouldn't stay there long, once he talked to Rum, they would probably be on the move again.

Meanwhile, in Birch Creek, the town was in a frenzy. Every inch of the town had been searched by the deputies and citizens. There was no sign of him and no evidence left. His disappearance felt like a black hole in the heart of this small town. Everyone was feeling uneasy. TJ, Ed and Reggie poured through recent files, trying to piece together any clues that might point to the sheriff's whereabouts.

"Whoever did this, knew what they were doing. No witnesses, no evidence. It's time to confront Nick." Reggie sounded determined.

"I will talk to the FBI about Nick's connection. Let them do their job, Reggie. TJ stated. "Ok, but I need to give them my input too."

"I agree." TJ said as he called the special agent.

CHAPTER 13

Nick had papers scattered across the table, looking for the perfect sculptures to order for the new park that would be finalized after the wedding but he was distracted. He was thinking about the text message he received from Rum. He didn't want to talk with Rum but he wondered what the consequences would be. He heard a knock at the door. Has Rum found him? He looked through the peephole in the door and saw two men that looked like police officers. His heart sank. He opened the door slightly.

"Can I help you?" He asked.

"Nick, we need to talk with you about the disappearance of Sheriff Johnson." The two men held up their FBI badges. Nick was caught off guard. He opened the door and let them in.

"Are you talking about the sheriff in Birch Creek?' Nick asked, feeling confused.

"Yes, we have reason to believe that you could be connected to his disappearance." The FBI agent had no expression. The other one was taking notes.

"Me? Why would I have something to do with someone I don't even know? I have heard his name through working with Reggie and TJ. I know he is part of her wedding party."

His stomach churned. He was thinking Rum had something to do with this. If he tells them anything about Rum, he will be killed.

"Nick, do you know Rumsfeld Mason?"

Here we go, he thought. He was trying to hold it together. "Yes, I do." He knew the FBI knew the answers already.

"Tell us how you know him." The agent taking notes looked up as the other one stared at him.

"He was my partner, we recently broke up." Nick was sweating at this point.

"What does this have to do with the disappearance of the sheriff?"

Nick asked, knowing all too well that Rum had probably directed Domino to kidnap him.

"You tell us."

"I don't know anything about this, I swear. "

After they asked several more questions which didn't bring any answers, they ended the interview.

"We will be back in touch with you very soon. We will probably take you down to our headquarters to record your interview. Don't leave town." The agent uttered.

"I have to go back to Birch Creek, I am the wedding planner and their wedding is in one week." He shouted.

"Don't you think the wedding may need to be postponed? Don't leave town." The agents walked towards the door leaving a business card on the table.

Nick ran to the bathroom to vomit. He sat on the bathroom floor wondering what to do. What has Rum done? He wants me to look like I had something to do with this. These are the consequences. The FBI knows I have connections to Rum. Why would Rum be targeting the sheriff? Is it because I refused to do the explosives so he had to change plans? It doesn't make sense. All of us who know Rum are in danger. Nick realized that Reggie and TJ must know by now that he knows Rum. He must call Reggie, they have worked so hard getting this wedding pulled together and now it may be postponed.

The FBI had already tapped Nick's phone. They wanted to see what his next move would be. They had discussed giving him enough information to let him know they knew he was connected to Rum. They achieved their mission for now but they had to gather evidence. An agent would be posted outside his building.

CHAPTER 14

Reggie and TJ had traveled back to St.Simons after rushing out during the night to Birch Creek when they got the news about the sheriff. Reggie stood in the kitchen staring at the half empty cup of tea in her hands. She felt empty and numb. TJ was leaning up against the counter, arms folded with a serious frown on his face. They were silent. Reggie jumped when her phone rang.

"It's Nick." She held her phone up showing TJ who was calling.

"Go ahead and answer, let's see what he has to say." TJ was clenching his jaw.

"Hello, Reggie. I wanted to talk with you and TJ."

"Nick, we have nothing to say to you, you are fired." Reggie was disgusted that he called. "Please wait, don't hang up. I am not sure what is going on but the FBI came to ask me questions about the sheriff disappearing. I knew nothing about it, I promise."

"Nick, TJ and I know you were with Rum for a long time. Whatever information you have about Rum should be told to the FBI. We realized that you must have been working with Rum to somehow hurt us."

"You hired me to be your wedding planner, remember? I was recommended by TJ's sister. I didn't seek you out. Please know that my plans for your wedding were to create a dream wedding for you and TJ." NIck was pacing and sounding defensive.

"I don't want to hear anything else you have to say." Reggie hung up the phone.

TJ knew what needed to happen as much he didn't want to say it.

"We have to postpone the wedding. Rum probably knew all the details about our wedding and could have been planning to destroy it somehow. He is more than likely responsible for the sheriff disappearing. We can't do anything until he is found."

Reggie quickly agreed and hugged TJ. She had already been thinking that she can't focus on a wedding right now. Again, silence filled the air after their decision settled over them. They could hear the waves hitting against the shoreline with the tide coming in. Sammy timed it perfectly to walk into the kitchen meowing and distract them from their heavy thoughts.

CHAPTER 15

A few days had passed since the kidnapping. Domino had to let the sheriff get up to eat, drink and use the bathroom. He had not heard back from Rum, after calling and texting him several times. He kept Sheriff Johnson blindfolded so he wouldn't be able to identify him. He talked as little as possible. Domino wouldn't answer any of the sheriff's questions.

Rum had gone silent. Maybe he had been found and arrested? He thought.

The citizens of Birch Creek had rallied again to continue searching for the sheriff. Mrs. Johnson was getting more worried as time passed. She knew her husband was smart and would try to get back home as quickly as possible. Ed and the rest of the team at the sheriff's office had notified all jurisdictions in the area to search for him too. Several of the surrounding counties had sent volunteers to help with the search. Ed would be the spokesperson for the department during the press conference to be held that afternoon. News and Radio stations had been notified and were already filling up the parking lot. It looked like a repeat of the press conferences that were held last year when all the women were missing. Ed saw people holding up signs and posters that read: *Where is our Sheriff? Bring him home safely* - Large photos of the sheriff were posted everywhere all over town.

When the press conference began, the parking lot was full from media trucks and concerned citizens. All law enforcement from Birch Creek and the surrounding counties were present to show a strong force presence.

Ed stepped up to the podium and adjusted the microphone. He cleared his throat. Mrs.

Johnson was standing just inside the building listening through the open doors. She didn't want to be seen in case the kidnappers were watching. Reggie and TJ couldn't get back to Birch Creek in time for the press conference so they were watching intently from their home.

"Ed looks nervous, which is expected. I can tell he is trying to hold it together." Reggie said as she glanced over at TJ. TJ didn't respond, his jaw tightening.

Ed began after the crowd quieted down.

"Our beloved Sheriff Johnson is missing. We are doing everything in our power to find him and bring him home safely. This is an ongoing investigation and we are asking the public to come forward if you have any information that could help us, you will remain anonymous if preferred. There are details we cannot share at this time."

The crowd started asking questions all at once. Ed held his hand up.

"One question at a time." He pointed to a reporter directly in front of him. "Deputy, Is there any indication of foul play involved?"

Ed hesitated and gripped the podium.

"Yes. At this time we are considering all possibilities. What I can say is that Sheriff Johnson is a deeply respected member of this community, and his absence is highly unusual. We are treating this matter with utmost urgency."

Another reporter spoke up when signaled by Ed.

"Are there any suspects? Could this be connected to the sheriff's work?"

"I cannot comment on potential suspects or motives at this time. We are not ruling anything out."

The questions continued but Ed cut the press conference short, urging everyone to respect the ongoing investigation.

Domino was clicking the remote repeatedly when he saw Ed standing at the podium giving a press conference. He turned up the muted volume. He leaned forward wanting to hear every word. He grabbed his cell phone to see if there was any word from Rum yet. No communication from Rum. When the press conference ended, he turned off the TV and went outside to smoke. He needs to think about what he will do if he doesn't hear from Rum soon. I can't just keep him here indefinitely. Should I let him go? I need a plan. He dialed Rum's number again. No answer. He left another message saying that he needed him to call back.

He threw the phone down when he walked back inside. He decided that if he didn't hear back from Rum by tomorrow then he would make his own move. He felt uneasy but wasn't going to get caught just because Rum is ghosting him.

Sheriff Johnson had remained calm during his captivity. He listened and had very little communication with his kidnapper. He figured out that his kidnapper was waiting on further instructions. He heard the press conference and realized the amount of resources that were pouring into his disappearance.

CHAPTER 16

Nick had seen the press conference too. He was convinced it had to be the work of Rum. He was certain Rum had ordered Domino to do it. Giving information about Domino would be very helpful and possibly be leverage for him to make a deal with the FBI. He was going to go to the FBI on his own before he was summoned to go. He looked at the card left by the agent and called the number listed on the card.

"This is Nick, I need to know how to find your office. I need to talk with you."

The agent gave him the office address. He contemplated if he should call his one and only friend at the moment, Betty. He decided not to involve her unless he was going to be arrested, then he would need to make arrangements for the apartment.

Nick arrived at the FBI headquarters. He was met at the front desk by the 2 agents that came to his apartment. They walked him to the elevator and up to the 4th floor. He was led into a conference room with cameras and 2 other agents present already seated. Nick couldn't stop his legs from shaking under the table. He was sweating.

"Nick, tell us what you know." The agent didn't want to make small talk, he cut right to the questions.

"First of all, I want to say that I know nothing about the disappearance of the sheriff in Birch Creek, I do have a strong feeling that Rum has something to do with it." He was taking some deep breaths.

"Tell us more, why do you think Rum has something to do with it?" The agent pushed on. "Rum found out that I was the hired wedding planner for Reggie and TJ and encouraged me to help him sabotage the wedding somehow. I refused to do what he wanted me to do. Rum was taking it too far."

"Keep going, what was he wanting you to do?"

"Rum was going to have explosives planted in the ceiling of the new pavilion that is being built for their wedding. He wanted me to be the one to trigger the explosives during the reception. I refused and realized that I can't continue to be with such an evil person." Nick was feeling relieved the more he talked and told them about Rum's plan.

"Why did he want to hurt all these people? Who was going to plant the explosives?" "He hates Reggie and all women for that matter. He wanted to give Reggie and the FBI something else to focus on besides trying to find him. He says there is no evidence to link him to any crimes. He is careful to make everyone else do the dirty work for him. I chose not to get involved in his business because I really didn't want to know what he was doing. I really don't have information about his trafficking. I know I made a bad choice to look the other way and stay with him for as long as I did. I felt somewhat trapped and scared to do anything. You asked who would be planting the explosives? That would be one of his employees named Domino. I feel sure Rum probably made Domino kidnap the sheriff."

"How do we find Domino? What's his last name and can you contact him?"

"I don't know how to find him nor do I know his name or how to contact him. Most of Rum's employees worked on ships or at the ports. Some of those employees you already put in jail could probably tell you how to find Domino. I am sure Domino had something to do with those girls who got kidnapped from Birch Creek last year."

Nick continued to tell the agents all about his relationship with Rum and how Rum manipulates everyone. He also reiterated how he knew he was now in danger after not carrying out his plan. Two of the agents had already left the room and Nick was sure they were following up on some of the information that he had already revealed. Nick was correct."

"Nick, if everything you are telling us is the truth, you won't be charged with anything. You made some very bad choices to look the other way but if you prevented people from being harmed and you helped us find the sheriff, Domino and Rum, then you can be protected."

Nick had tears in his eyes. He finally felt free and relieved. He wondered if the FBI was really being honest with him or not. He had to trust the process.

"Nick, you may just be the link that ties all of this together. If so, Rum will be in prison for the rest of his life and you may save a lot of lives or save others from being abused. Again, don't leave town, we will probably need to ask you some more questions once we follow up. We need to know how to find you."

"Ok, I have to admit that I am really scared of what Rum will do to me."

"We will have agents posted outside your apartment building and inside as well."

Nick left and couldn't believe he had been interviewed for 4 hours. He was exhausted but felt lighter after revealing everything.

CHAPTER 17

Domino was pacing the floor the next morning knowing he had to move soon. He had no reason to keep the sheriff and didn't understand why Rum wanted him kidnapped in the first place but he had learned to not ask questions. If Rum has disappeared or been caught then he doesn't need to be found with the sheriff. He went outside to smoke before he would make his next move. He ran a hand over his face, his stubble was rough against his palm. It had been days since he had heard from Rum. No texts, No calls. Just radio silence. That wasn't normal. Now, with every hour that passed, the situation grew more dangerous. Domino knew he had followed orders until the orders stopped coming. And that press conference...

The mayor, the police chief and even the Governor were all demanding answers. His mind raced, he had to do something. He had to let the sheriff go. Quietly, somewhere far enough from here. Domino grabbed the keys to the van, his stomach twisting. If he made the wrong move now, he was as good as dead. But if he waited any longer, he would already be caught.

"Get up, sheriff. We are going for a ride."

The sheriff climbed in the back of the van without talking. He wasn't sure if this was good or bad news. He was weak, stiff from not moving around much and his hip was really hurting at this point. He was nervous as time passed slowly while riding to an unknown destination. After what seemed like hours, the van stopped. Domino opened the back door. He pulled the sheriff's arm to help him get out, eyes still covered. The first thing Sheriff

Johnson felt was the cold, fresh air. It was a stark contrast to the stale, suffocating air of his captivity. His knees ached as he stumbled forward.

As the sheriff stood waiting for the next command, Domino stood behind him, cut him loose and told him not to take the blindfold off.

"You are free. Don't take the blindfold off until I drive away. I will be watching and I will have to shoot if you take the blindfold off."

"I understand. Thank you for letting me go. I will not take it off until you have driven away." Sheriff Johnson couldn't believe it was almost over. He heard the door slam shut and the van drove away. He took off the blind fold and looked around. For the first time in days, his eyes were open, but the world was a blur. It was too bright as he tried to focus on his surroundings. He was standing in an empty parking lot. He was in Atlanta, the gold dome on the Capitol Building was shining in the distance. He was alive and free. His heart pounded. His throat was raw, his muscles weak, every movement sent a dull ache through his bones. He spotted a gas station down on the corner of the street. He didn't spot any security cameras in the parking lot. The kidnapper was smart to pick this spot, he thought.

He slowly made his way across the parking lot, down the embankment and crossed the street. He entered the store, clothes dirty, limping, squinting his eyes. A young cashier looked up.

"Sir, are you ok?" She steps back nervously. The sheriff grips the counter, his voice is hoarse.

"I need you to call 911."

The cashier grabs her cell phone. She doesn't hesitate, she knows something is wrong but not sure what it is.

"Yeah, I got a man here who needs help. I'm not sure what has happened. It's the Quick stop on the corner, yes that's it."

The sheriff knew help was on the way, he leaned against the counter, hip hurting.

"Can I get you some water or something?" the store clerk asked.

"Thank you, yes, water."

As Domino drove away, his phone rang, "unknown number." Against his better judgement, he answers it.

"You just made a big mistake." The voice isn't familiar. "Who is this, what are you talking about?" Domino asked.

"You let the sheriff go, do you have any idea what you just did?"

"Rum wasn't responding, I had no orders and they were going to find me with him. I had no idea if Rum had been found or what happened. Who is this?" he asked again.

"Now, Rum knows you are unreliable, You're done, Domino. We will take it from here." The call ends. Domino grips the steering wheel. That must have been a test, one of Rum's games he plays. They must be close by. What will they do?

Domino turns the van around to head back to the parking lot. He sees a black SUV pulling into the nearby gas station. That must be them. He has a decision to make.

The sheriff sees a black SUV pull into the gas station. Two men step out standing close to their doors on each side of the SUV. The sheriff notices one man speaking into an ear piece. Something is wrong, the sheriff could feel it. They aren't the FBI.

"Lock the doors, he yells to the cashier." She runs to lock the doors, and calls 911 again.

"I don't know what's happening here but something is about to go down. Please hurry." She pleads with the 911 operator.

The two men try to open the store's front doors. The sheriff can hear the cashier talking to the 911 operator.

"These men are trying to get in. I locked the door." she screams.

All of sudden, the white van, the kidnapper, pulls up. The sheriff had seen a glimpse of the van as it drove away when he was released. Domino jumps out. Pointing a gun at the two men.

"Back off." Domino yells.

"You're too late, we got this." One of the men yells back.

"Not happening." Domino grips the gun.

"You know what happens if you get in Rum's way." One of the men says sternly.

The sheriff could hear the exchange. It is Rum ordering all of this. Why did the kidnapper come back to help him? Or is he here to help? He could hear the sirens in the background getting closer.

The two men exchange glances at each other, they can hear the sirens too.

"You just signed your death warrant, Domino."

They jump back in the SUV and take off. Domino does the same, he drives off in his van. The sheriff now knows his kidnappers name and knows that Rum is behind all of this. The police arrive, the clerk unlocks the doors and starts explaining what happened.

"Sir, are you ok?" One of the officers asks.

"I need to talk to the FBI now. I am sheriff Johnson from Birch Creek. I was kidnapped days ago."

"Right away, sir. Let's take you to the station and call the FBI and your team in Birch Creek." He was going home, finally.

Domino was now a fugitive. The FBI and Rum's men would be hunting him down. He also realized the FBI would be hunting down Rum and his men. Rum's men made a critical mistake using his name. He heard it, the sheriff probably heard it, and he knows the store had cameras recording too. He needed to withdraw enough cash to stay missing for a while. He also needed to ditch the van and get a different vehicle. He withdrew cash and left the van at a nearby park. He left on foot. He could hide out in the city for a while.

CHAPTER 18

The sheriff had been home for a couple of weeks now. He had recovered, back on duty. Reggie and TJ had visited him to make sure he was ok. Reggie's consulting role with the FBI was going to help put Rum away for good. Reggie had talked with the FBI agent who met with Nick and interviewed the sheriff at length about his kidnapper. Domino was his name. She knew that Nick had to know Domino too.

TJ and Reggie were back at their home, with security detail posted outside. The case files were everywhere. Papers covered the dining table, maps covered the wall with red marker lines connecting names and locations. A whiteboard in the corner was filled with theories.

TJ stood in the doorway watching Reggie. She sat at the table reading over the sheriff's statement for the hundredth time. She wasn't sleeping or eating right. Her mind was focused on finding Rum. She was drowning in all the facts with no idea where to find Rum. The last time he saw her in this state was back in Birch Creek when she was the only detective in that small town trying to solve the crime of the missing girls.

"Reggie."

She didn't look up.

"I'm missing something. Rum's not stupid. He wouldn't just disappear without a plan. He's waiting, but for what?"

She grabbed her notebook and started scribbling. TJ saw her grip tighten as she tapped the pen on the paper.

"Reggie, stop."

She finally looked up at him.

"I can't stop, TJ. Rum is still out there. Until he is caught, we're all targets. The sheriff barely made it home. What if next time it's someone else?" What if it's..."

She stopped in mid sentence. And that's when TJ knew. Reggie wasn't just obsessed with the case, she was scared. But she wouldn't let herself feel scared, instead she would bury herself in the work, not stopping until he was found.

"Reggie, listen to me. You're too close to this. You need to take a step back." Reggie immediately was shaking her head no.

"No, I need to figure this out." "And you will but not like this."

She looked up again. He had her attention.

"You're not eating, you're not sleeping. Hell, when was the last time you walked out to the beach or left the house?"

"I'm fine." She folded her arms in front of her. She got that stubborn look on her face. "No, you're not."

Reggie was glaring at him, knowing he was right but not going to give in. She was tired but couldn't possibly rest. She grabbed the sheriff's statement, reading it over again.

"I'm going for a walk." TJ yelled as he walked out the back door, slamming it shut.

Reggie knew he slammed it on purpose to make his point. He was mad.

As he walked along the beach, the night air was cool. The waves were calm. No one else in sight on the beach. He thought about what his father said when he visited them. The ocean reminds you how life keeps moving and you need to focus on what really matters. Time will slip by without us realizing it. He decided he needed to take matters into his own hands. He and Reggie needed to get married without all the fuss of a wedding. They don't need time to slip by. He also decided he would do his own investigating behind the scenes.

When he got back to the house, Reggie wasn't sitting at the table. He walked into their bedroom, she was actually asleep. Sammy was laying at her feet. His talk must have done some good or either she was just so exhausted she couldn't stay awake. He walked out on the back deck. He sat down with a glass of bourbon. He scrolled through his contacts on his phone. He found Nick's number, looked at it for a few minutes, then took a deep breath and pressed call. The phone rang at least 4 times and when TJ was about to hang up Nick answered.

"Hello?" Nick's voice sounded hesitant and sleepy.

"It's about Rum." TJ waited on a response.

"What about him?"

"You tell me, you know him better than anyone, if he's gone underground, where the hell is he?"

"If I knew, I would have told the FBI so I could rest easier. I have a target on my head too." "Any ideas or speculations at this point?"

"I can speculate all day long but that's all it is. Rum doesn't just vanish. He's waiting for something."

TJ clenched his jaw. He already knew the answer but he needed to hear it. "Waiting for what?"

"Not what, who."

TJ closed his eyes. Reggie.

"Rum's always 3 steps ahead. He had backup plans for his backup plans. The fact that no one has seen him? That's intentional. He's making people think he's gone so they'll let their guard down."

"And then what?"

"He will finish what he started." Nick exhaled.

TJ was silent on the other end. Nick thought he might have hung up. TJ let out a big sigh. "Knowing him he is hiding in plain sight."

TJ wasn't sure if Nick knew the FBI had confirmed it was Rum who ordered the kidnapping and it was Domino who kidnapped the sheriff. He still wasn't trusting of him so he wasn't going to give him information.

"Rum's not like other criminals. He doesn't run. He resets. He disappears just enough to make people think he's gone, but he's still watching. Still controlling everything from a distance."

TJ swallowed hard.

"Then he's got to be stopped before he makes his next move. I'm not waiting around for him to come after Reggie."

TJ hung up. The call ended but the words lingered in his head.

"He doesn't run, he resets."

He no longer has Domino doing his dirty work and it's just a matter of time before the FBI catches those other 2 men. Rum blames Reggie for his downfall and ruining his operation. He may want to destroy her himself if he has no one left. TJ had to come up with a plan quickly.

CHAPTER 19

Domino had hitched a ride to Lexington, Kentucky. He had a friend who would loan him a car and some cash. His friend owed him from a job Domino did for him years ago. He was staying in a hotel close to the highway, where he could pay with cash and no one asked questions. Domino's friend showed up the next morning, knocking loudly which finally made Domino wake up. He was more tired than he had realized. Money was given to him but the car wouldn't be ready to pick up for a few more days. It was being painted and the license plate changed. Domino asked that food be brought to him, he didn't want to chance being seen outside. Too many cameras are around.

For the next couple of days, all Domino could do was think about what his plans for the future will be. Should he help the FBI find Rum? Should he go to see Nick? Should he leave the country? He is a fugitive who will be charged with kidnapping, unless he makes a deal with the FBI. He had to weigh all his options. Rum will have him killed. He watched the news constantly wanting to know if there was a manhunt for him. He wasn't seeing any news stories about Sheriff Johnson returning home or any news stories about Rum. As he contemplated on what his next move should be, he realized he couldn't go see Nick. The FBI would be all over him. He can't leave the country, his face was recorded on the store's video camera. He needs to talk to the FBI and find Rum. He had to think like Rum. What would Rum do? Rum would be wanting revenge for anyone who betrays him. He would still be after Reggie, Nick and now him. Rum won't give up even if he doesn't have anyone to do his dirty work. He would find Rum and turn him in. Once his friend brings him the car, he will be heading to Birch Creek again.

Rum's house on the mountain may have some clue as to where Rum would go next. Domino knows how to get in and could actually hide out there for a while.

CHAPTER 20

TJ stayed up most of the night coming up with his plan. He kept thinking about what Nick told him. *"Rum resets, he might be hiding in plain sight."* Where does one go to reset? TJ thought about how he would go home to reset. Maybe Rum is at his home in Birch Creek.

Reggie slept until 8am which was very unusual for her. She had finally crashed from exhaustion. She woke up feeling rested but confused.

"Did you not sleep in the bed with me last night?" She asked TJ.

"No, I wanted you to sleep and I was up most of the night thinking about us and this Rum issue. We don't need Rum controlling us - We have postponed our wedding due to him being so damn crazy! I won't have it anymore. We need to get married without making a big announcement and not worrying about all the grand ceremony stuff."

"I like what we had planned, I don't want to change it. What do you have in mind?" Reggie knew they couldn't go forward with everything they had planned because Nick was no longer planning it.

"We can still get married at the chapel and have the reception by the river, we just don't need it publicized. Kind of like the spur of the moment."

"I'm fine with that, it's just not that moment, yet." She smiled and grabbed his hand.

" I know, I have things to take care of first anyway." TJ was going to find Rum and get him out of their lives once and for all. He was headed to Birch

Creek, to Rum's home on the mountain. If he is there, TJ will find him and have him arrested.

"Tomorrow, I have some business to take care of and I'm going to go check on how the pavilion is coming along. I will drive up there." TJ didn't want Reggie to know his plans because she would try to stop him.

"Do you want me to go with you?"

"No, you stay here and finish working on what you feel you need to do." Reggie wasn't wanting to go this time because all she could focus on was this investigation. She was relieved he told her to stay home.

TJ would leave early in the morning before Reggie woke up. He took a long walk along the beach to think about and finalize his plan.

CHAPTER 21

TJ kissed Reggie's forehead and whispered, I love you. Sammy was laying at the foot of the bed, he lifted his head, acknowledging TJ. TJ smiled knowing Sammy would probably be in the same spot when he returned home. TJ wasn't sure when he would return home. He might have to go somewhere else depending on what he finds out. He was a man determined to protect the love of his life. He told the security guards to stay there with her. He explained he was driving himself up to Birch Creek and didn't need security tagging along. He told them he had protection, as he patted his bag laying in the seat.

It took several hours to drive up to Birch Creek which gave TJ time to think about his future with Reggie. He was happy, he wanted to show her the world and create lots of wonderful memories with her. Rum needs to be in prison for all the horrible things he has done and made others do. His trafficking network was dwindling which could be completely demolished and that could save so many lives and so many people from abuse. When TJ arrived in Birch Creek, he drove over to see the construction work being done on the pavilion. He had instructed the builder that they could slow down a bit in building it due to the postponement of the wedding.

When he arrived, it looked like they were almost finished with the pavilion. They were grading for the amphitheater. He would contact someone new to find some sculpture pieces to be placed throughout the park. He would also commission someone to make a sign for the new "Purple Mountains Majesty Park." TJ felt good, this was right, everything felt right. He talked briefly with the landscaper before leaving. He had to drive up the mountain before dark.

After turning at the Rock Church, he forgot how quickly the road turned to gravel and dirt.

He was driving along the winding road realizing he had never been up the road past Rum's property. Today would be the day, he would see more of the mountain, he had to figure out how to get into Rum's property, possibly from the back side. He had studied the property lines yesterday when making his plans. He knew there would be a road that parallels the property line on the rear side. As he traveled up the winding road, there was no one in sight, he had not passed a single car. We drove up the road past the gate of Rum's property. The road got more narrow with no gravel, just dirt. After a couple of miles, he saw the access road that he thought must be the one that would lead him to the rear of Rum's property. He knew he would have to park his car and walk up the steep hill to find Rum's property. He was prepared, he had dressed properly with his hiking boots, hoody and his bag. He pulled the car into what seemed to be a turn around spot along the side of the road. He parked, and checked his phone. No fucking cell service! He knew if he sees Rum, he won't be able to call law enforcement until he reaches cell service back down the mountain. TJ hiked up the hill moving carefully with the leaves crunching under his boots. He was stepping on twigs and leaves and flinching at every sound they made.

He knew he wasn't comfortable with this scene, the hill, the uneven trail, the stillness of the dark. But none of that mattered, not tonight. He saw an orange flag that looked like a marker for a property line. He couldn't believe that the rear side of Rum's property wasn't the huge fence he had along the front and sides, it was barbed wire. Easy to crawl through and sneak a peek at Rum's house. He was careful to stay out of sight, He knew Rum only had cameras around his house but not at the front gate and hopefully not all the way back here in the woods. It was starting to get darker now and in the dense wood, no sunlight was peeking through. A low fog drifted across the ground curling up around the trees. He could tell the temperature had dropped too, being up on this elevation. TJ was not used to hiking in the woods, he was nervously listening to all the sounds coming from around him. He paused, listening. A distant sound, like a rustling, maybe an animal, maybe not. He could see in the distance a light. That had to be a light on at Rum's house. He ducked under a large twisted branch squinting to see. Could he be there or maybe has a timer that turns lights on and off when he is away? TJ wasn't quite sure what he was going to do next except keep moving closer to the house and then watch, listen and wait. He had some binoculars in his bag but it was getting too dark to see with them. He kept sneaking closer. He could see lights coming from 2 areas of the house. One light was a huge spotlight on the side corner outside of the house, close to the garage area.

Another was a light coming from inside. He guessed it was coming from the living room because there were glass doors leading out to the patio. He crouched down and waited. After a few minutes, he was certain there was no one home. All of a sudden when he was about to give up, he saw the light flicker as if someone walked past it. His heart started beating faster, someone was inside. Please let it be Rum, he thought to himself. If it is then we got him! This was it, the end of the chase.

CHAPTER 22

TJ was sweating, adrenaline was on overload, he was driving as fast as he could down the winding road of the mountain. He kept looking at his phone, still no cell service. He was breathing hard, it seemed like the longest 5 miles of his life driving down that dirt road. Finally he reached the pavement and pulled in the parking lot at the Rock Church. He called Sheriff Johnson directly, by-passing 911.

"Sheriff Johnson, Rum is dead! He is dead!" TJ was yelling, taking deep breaths so he didn't vomit.

"TJ, is that you? What are you talking about? Where are you?"

"I'm at the Rock Church parking lot. I went up the mountain to see if Rum was there. And he was there but he is dead. He was lying in the kitchen."

"Stay there, we are on the way. I have to call the FBI." Sheriff Johnson hung up.

TJ got out of the car, pacing, breathing- "Reggie, I need to call Reggie." He sat back in the car and called her.

"Reggie, Rum is dead. I am here in Birch Creek, I saw him dead at his house."

"Wait, what? TJ, are you sure? I don't understand what you are telling me. You were at his house?" Reggie was trying to let the news sink in. She had so many questions.

"I'm waiting at the Rock Church, Sheriff Johnson and the FBI are on their way. I will tell you the whole story later. I have to go, they are arriving."

He hung up with Reggie in disbelief. Did she hear him right, is it true? She heard the sirens when he was hanging up. She walked into the kitchen to get her keys thinking she needed to leave now and drive up to Birch Creek. No, she would wait to hear back from TJ. She felt helpless wondering what had he seen and why on earth was he at his house. And how did he know to go up there? She looked at the time, it was almost midnight. Her hands were shaking, she realized she was pacing around her house. She made some coffee, it would be a long night.

TJ rode with Sheriff Johnson up the mountain. Several deputies and the FBI were following them.

"TJ, I don't know why you were up here all alone trying to find Rum. That should be left up to us and the FBI. Whatever your story is, you better have it straight because you are going to be questioned not only by me but the FBI and don't forget Reggie too."

"Sheriff, I had a feeling he was up here hiding out. He was making our lives miserable. Reggie can't think about anything else and I didn't want to put our lives on hold any longer. I can't believe he is dead." TJ was running on adrenaline, but mentally tired. He knew he had some answers to give.

"I don't want to question you about what you saw until we get inside his house, no confusion, no assumptions, just facts." As they reached the entrance gate, it was open.

"Why is the gate open?"

"I don't know. It was closed when I came up here. I drove around the back side of his property on an old access road."

"Then how did you get into his house?" the sheriff was shaking his head, not wanting to know the answer.

"I walked up through the woods. I know it was wrong but I had to know if he was there."

As they entered through the gate, the long driveway winds down towards the hidden house. The landscaping was pristine as if just freshly planted. TJ had not seen the front side of Rum's house, it looked bigger from the front than the back. The deputies and FBI surrounded the house, guns drawn. Sheriff Johnson told TJ to wait in the car until someone comes out to get him. They needed to secure the scene and look around. The massive front door was unlocked. A deputy was following along with the sheriff who was telling him to take notes. The deputies had already cleared and secured the scene before the FBI and the sheriff entered.

The entrance gate was open at his arrival. The front door was unlocked. No signs of forced entry. Sheriff Johnson stepped inside, his instincts immediately on edge. He moved slowly, eyes scanning the hallway, nothing seemed disturbed. No toppled furniture, no broken glass, no blood. He hoped the deputy was logging all of it, though his gut told him the scene wouldn't stay quiet for long. Then he stepped into the kitchen. The air was thick with the scent of blood. The tiled floor, once a pale beige, was smeared deep red around the lifeless body of Rum. FBI agents moved with precision. Cameras clicked, evidence bags filled, voices low, Sheriff Johnson's eyes narrowed as he took it all in. No weapon visible. No indication of a fight.

Whatever happened here, it had been fast, clean and cold. He felt the weight of it all settle in his chest. This was the man who ordered him to be kidnapped. Sheriff Johnson remained still and silent for a moment. He looked at Rum's body. It was motionless, eyes opened, mouth slightly opened as if he was talking when the fatal shot hit.

"Sheriff," one of the agents caught his attention.

"We'll need a statement from you too since Mr. Jenkins called you first and rode with you back here to the crime scene." The sheriff nodded in agreement. He then turned and made his way back through the pristine hallway, each step heavy with the questions piling up in his mind.

TJ sat in the front seat of the patrol car, motionless, except tapping his fingers on his leg.

He stared straight ahead. Sheriff Johnson knew the shock of it all had not worn off.

"TJ, are you ready to come in and tell us what you observed?" Sheriff Johnson asked as he opened his car door.

"I observed exactly what you just saw. Rum laying in the kitchen, dead." "You found him just like that?" he asked.

"Yes."

"TJ, when we go in, I need you to take your time and start from the beginning. You will show the FBI where you entered, etc. Then you will be interviewed again when we return to my office. It's going to be a long night."

They entered through the front door. One of the FBI agents was taking the lead now. "Start from here at this point." the agent paused.

"I can't start from here because I was never in this part of the house. I came in the back patio door." TJ's adrenaline was still running high.

"I came through the back, up the mountain trail. I would not have been able to enter from the front."

"Why were you looking for him, exactly?" The agent raised his eyebrows from just learning TJ had sneaked in from the back. TJ swallowed hard.

"I needed to see him, face to face. After everything he did to Reggie, to all of us...I just needed to know if he was here, hiding in plain sight. I wanted you all to arrest him." His voice trembled. Sheriff Johnson nodded. The agent continued:

"And when you got close to the house?"

"I saw the light flicker as if someone moved past it." "But you kept going?"

"I had to," TJ said, his voice firmer now. "I stepped onto the back porch. The door wasn't even latched. I called his name once and then went in. And then....he hesitated, I saw him."

Sheriff Johnson studied him in silence. Something is his gut shifted. The details lined up but it was too neat, too clean and TJ was calm now. But he said nothing. Instead, he walked outside for a minute to think. Something wasn't adding up, not yet.

The FBI agent nodded for TJ to keep going explaining what happened next.

"When I saw him....when I realized he was dead, I froze for a second. I didn't know what to do. I just knew I had to get help."

Sheriff Johnson entered back into the room.

"I ran back out the way I came through the woods, got to my car as fast as I could. I didn't even think about checking the rest of the house. I just wanted out."

The agent kept his expression neutral, jotting down notes. "And then?"

TJ's voice steadied slightly, like he was back into the moment.

"I jumped in the car and started down the mountain. I didn't have any cell signal so I kept driving until I got to the Rock Church where I knew I could get service. That's when I finally got a signal and called the sheriff."

Johnson nodded.

"Did you see anyone else? Any cars, anyone on the trail?" TJ shook his head quickly.

"No, it was dead quiet, no one else was around." "You're sure?" he asked, voice low.

TJ finally looked him straight in the eye. "I'm sure."

For a long moment, there was silence. No one spoke. The other agents were moving about the house.

"Alright, we will need to get your formal statement recorded back at the office." TJ and the sheriff both nodded in agreement.

CHAPTER 23

They returned to the small Birch Creek office and sat in the conference room. Sheriff Johnson, the FBI agent and TJ sat around the table, coffee in hand. A digital recorder sat in the center of the table. They could hear the others outside talking but it remained quiet there. TJ sat stiffly in the chair, tired, ready to get the interview over and go home.

"Ok, tell me again what you told me, where exactly you found the body." TJ cleared his throat.

"In the kitchen, near the sink. He was lying facedown...blood everywhere. I could smell it the second I stepped inside."

"You didn't touch anything?"

"No," TJ said quickly. "I didn't even go further into the room. As soon as I saw him, I backed out and ran."

"Are you certain you didn't see anyone else?" TJ tightened his jaw, "No one."

Sheriff Johnson leaned back slightly, studying him. After a few more routine questions, verifying the time he left home, the route he took and the time lapse from when he called the sheriff.

"That's all for now, We'll be in touch." The agent offered a hand shake to TJ and the sheriff. "I need to call Reggie, I'm sure she is beside herself."

"We'll get out so you can have some time to talk to her." Sheriff Johnson closed the door as they walked out.

TJ's hands shook as he pressed the button to call Reggie. It had been a long night. She answered on the second ring.

"TJ, where are you? What's going on? Are you ok?" She was frantic.

TJ closed his eyes, taking a deep breath, embracing himself against the wave of questions coming at him.

"I'm ok. I promise. I found Rum dead like I told you earlier. I went to his house in Birch Creek on the mountain."

"Found him dead?" she asked.

"He's dead, Reggie. I called the sheriff right away, "The FBI is handling everything now." The silence on the line was heavy and sharp.

"How?" She finally whispered.

TJ rubbed his head, his heart was pounding.

"I don't know," he said. "When I found him, he was already gone. It looked....bad. But I swear I didn't see anyone else."

Reggie was quiet again.

"Are you sure you're okay?" She asked with her voice cracking just a little.

"I'm fine," TJ lied. "I just need you to trust me on this. Everything's gonna be okay now. We can finally move on."

He meant it, they could finally move on.

"TJ, You have been up all night, do I need to come get you?"

"No, I'm going to sleep a couple of hours here in your old office on the sofa and then head home to you."

"Ok, I have lots of questions but I know you have to be exhausted. We can talk when you get home."

Reggie stood frozen in the middle of her kitchen, the phone pressed to her chest. She could hear the ocean waves crashing against the rocks as the tide came in. She finally lowered the phone, setting it carefully on the counter as if it might shatter. Dead. Rum was dead. And TJ had been the one to find him. A tremor ran through her as she leaned back against the counter for support. Part of her felt like she should be relieved. Rum was dead and maybe they could finally breathe. No more fear of what he would do next. But something about TJ's voice stuck in her mind. Too calm, too careful. She shook the thought away, scolding herself. Of course he was in shock. Of course he was trying to hold it together for her. She knew TJ. She trusted him. Still, she had a feeling tightening in her chest, one she couldn't quite loosen. She turned and stared out the kitchen window toward the ocean. She then turned to look at the papers scattered all over her table that she had been sorting through hoping to find a clue as to where to find Rum and put him in prison for life. And now, just like that, he is dead. Rum is dead. She wondered who knew this information. Did Nick know yet? This would be big news all over the media, the head of the largest human trafficking network is now dead. Once the FBI releases this news to the press, Birch Creek will be crowded with news crews again.

CHAPTER 24

A few days had passed since the incident. TJ was home, it was late at night. He stared up at the ceiling fan whirling above. Reggie was sleeping beside him. They could now plan their wedding again. It was all over and going to be ok. He lay there with his eyes wide open in the dark. He could hear Sammy purring and feel his paws on his leg. No sleep for him. He couldn't clear his mind. He had not heard any more updates regarding the investigation of Rum's death except for what the media was reporting. No word from Sheriff Johnson. Reggie had asked him questions over and over which he expected. He knew she was disappointed that he had not told her where he was going when he left to go look for Rum. He had envisioned finding him at his Birch Creek Mountain home, then calling in the FBI to arrest him. He predicted seeing Rum there but never predicted seeing him dead. He had briefly talked with Nick a couple of days ago. Nick had questioned him too about going after Rum.

TJ had just fallen asleep when Reggie's phone was ringing. She jumped, reaching for the phone right away.

"Hello? Oh hey, are you ok? What time is it?"

TJ could only hear one side of the conversation but quickly realized it was Sheriff Johnson that Reggie was talking too. Reggie sat up in bed and was silent. The sun was coming up and peeking in the gap between the closed curtains. Reggie looked back at him, quickly standing up.

"Ok, whatever we need to do. We can leave within a couple of hours." She said goodbye in a soft voice.

"TJ, we have to go back to Birch Creek this morning. The FBI has more questions for you and wants to interview you in person again."

"Why? I have told them all I know. Can they come here?" TJ asked. He was tired and wanted to stay home.

"I can ask. I know you haven't been sleeping well. Let me call the sheriff back."

Reggie went into the kitchen to make coffee. She sipped her coffee looking out at the beautiful morning. The sun was shining on the water and as if on cue, the dolphin fins rose above the water. She took a deep breath, taking in the beauty and feeling so thankful. She dialed Sheriff Johnson.

"Hey, we were wondering if the FBI agent could come here to interview TJ again? He is so tired and hasn't been sleeping."

"He needs to come here. They want to video his interview again. Reggie, they haven't found any evidence and have no leads."

"What are you saying? Is he a suspect?" Reggie's voice was shaking.

"Reggie, you know how this works. They had to look at all the evidence and talk to anyone who was at the scene."

"Does he need to bring his attorney?"

"Reggie, that is up to TJ. If he wants an attorney with him, then he should bring his attorney. I can't advise you on this." Sheriff Johnson was worried about how this situation may turn out.

"Ok, we may need more than a day to arrange travel for his attorney. I will be in touch."

TJ walked in the kitchen just as Reggie was hanging up the call. TJ noticed right away that something was wrong.

"What is it?" He asked.

"I think you should call your attorney. The FBI wants to video your interview again. They have no leads and you were the person at the scene. I told the sheriff we may need more than a day to arrange travel. Is there anything you haven't told them?" She raised her eyebrow looking at TJ.

"I will call my attorney now and make arrangements. We can go as soon as possible. I want to get all of this behind us. Reggie, I just wanted to help find him and put him in prison. That's it."

CHAPTER 25

They arrived in Birch Creek with TJ's attorney that same afternoon. TJ didn't want to waste any more time on this.

"Let's get this interview over with." He said as they entered the room with the FBI agents.

Reggie was asked to leave the room.

Reggie knew she wouldn't be allowed in the room. She went down the hall to find Ed. He would occupy her while the interview was in process.

TJ sat at the table with his attorney seated beside him. His attorney was calm, polished, one hand resting on a closed legal pad. Across the table, two FBI agents reviewed their notes.

"For the record, this is the voluntary interview of Mr. Terrence J. Jenkins, present with counsel, regarding the investigation into the death of Rumsfeld Mason. The time is 1600 hours." He glanced briefly at TJ.

"Mr. Jenkins, you understand you are not under arrest and you are here voluntarily?" "My client understands." His attorney spoke up quickly.

"Mr. Jenkins tell us approximately what time you arrived at Rum's house and why were you there?"

"I am not sure what time it was, it was getting dark, The woods seemed darker because of the fog rolling in. It had to be right before sundown. I was there hoping to find Rum. I wanted to find him, turn him in and watch him go to prison."

"Describe what you saw when you entered the house." The agent leaned in. Eyes fixed on watching TJ's body movements and listening intently. TJ described the scene again just as he had done 2 times already. After he finished, his attorney stood up.

"My client has explained everything and cooperates fully in this ongoing investigation. At this time, I would like to end this interview due to this not being an interrogation."

"We agree. If we have further questions, we can call." The agent looked at the other one for his approval. They all shook hands and TJ and his attorney left the room. TJ pulled his attorney aside in the parking lot before Reggie came out to meet them. His attorney was on his cell phone telling his assistant which cases to reference for him when he returns.

"Look, I know how this looks but they can't pin this on me. Maybe they are looking at others from Rum's past but it doesn't seem that way right now." TJ leaned against the car, hands in his pockets fidgeting with the car keys.

"Don't worry, they just want to be sure about everything you have told them. I can suggest they look into others. It's going to be ok. Let me reference some previous cases and study my strategy if that is needed."

Reggie came out to the car with the Sheriff close behind her. "How did it go?' She asked.

"I told them the story again, that's it. They seemed satisfied with my details."

"Well, good. Let's go home and plan our wedding!" Reggie grabbed his hand smiling at Sheriff Johnson.

"Sounds like a good idea to me." Sheriff Johnson shook TJ's hand, then hugged Reggie.

"Call me if you need anything." he waved bye as they backed out.

CHAPTER 26

Reggie and TJ were feeling relieved at the thoughts of getting on with their future plans.

They still wanted to get married at the Birch Creek Chapel as planned. The pavilion was finished, landscaping was being completed. TJ had commissioned an artist from Chicago to do the park sculptures, which were to be installed in a couple of weeks. A sign was being made that would be installed at the front of the path leading to the pavilion. *"Purple Mountains Majesty Park,"* dedicated to all Birch Creek citizens. Reggie was ordering flowers and candles to place on each of the tables for the reception. They decided to have their wedding in the spring to give time for the park to look even more beautiful.

"Reggie, let's go walk on the beach, and discuss where we want to go on our honeymoon." TJ pulled her up from the sofa, kissing her forehead as she moved closer upon rising.

"Alright, let's go somewhere you have never been."

"You think I have traveled all over the world and really I haven't. I think Ireland in the spring would be nice." They held hands walking out to the beach.

"Ireland, she sighed. I have never thought about going there but yes, that sounds amazing. I need to learn more about it and see what we can do there."

"Reggie, we have a travel agent that can plan everything for us. You don't need to do anything except marry me and pack your bags." He smiled knowing she isn't used to having others do planning or anything else for her.

"Ok, let's do it."

"I will call the travel agent today." TJ squeezed her hand slightly, feeling the excitement too.

As they walked back in the house, TJ scooped Reggie up in his arms carrying her to the bed. He slowly undressed her, not taking his eyes off hers. She felt his warm body on her, making her have that tingling feeling inside. She loved this man. They made love satisfying each other with even greater pleasure than ever before. They were happy, content and moving on without the thoughts of needing to fear Rum Mason.

Reggie pulled on her robe as soon as she heard her cell phone ringing. TJ was in the shower already waiting for her to join him.

"Hey Sheriff, how are you?"

"Reggie, I'm calling to tell you the FBI is on their way to your house to arrest TJ. I tried calling you earlier, glad I finally reached you."

"Arrest him? They think he murdered Rum?" Reggie was pacing trying to figure out what to do.

"I need to tell TJ and call his attorney. I will call you later, thanks for telling me." She hung up. The doorbell rang. Her heart sank. The FBI agents were standing at her front door.

TJ had showered and dressed when he appeared in the foyer. "What's going on? Who is at the door?"

"It's the FBI, they are here to arrest you." Her eyes filled with tears. TJ opened the front door.

"Come in." He stepped out of the way for them to enter.

"Terrence Jenkins, you are under arrest for the murder of Rumsfeld Mason. Turn around, please." TJ turned and let them handcuff him. He took a deep breath, slowly letting out the air.

Two FBI agents stood on each side, one reading him his rights. TJ stood still, head lowered. He didn't argue, he didn't resist. His heart was beating fast as they loaded him into the back of the car. Once the doors were shut, he looked up at Reggie standing in disbelief looking at him. He smiled at her trying to reassure her in this fragile moment.

CHAPTER 27

Reggie stood frozen on the front steps, her heart pounding against her ribs. TJ had said nothing. He just glanced up in her direction with a smile that she knew was only meant for her. Now, the car was pulling away, tail lights blinking as she watched them pull out onto the street. She didn't move, she couldn't move. She felt like the wind had been knocked out of her. TJ arrested for murder. The words didn't make sense. They didn't fit the man she knew. The man who had stood by her side through every piece of the Rum ordeal, who had promised they were finally safe, that it was over. She reached for the railing to steady herself. She knew this was a mistake, why didn't he say anything or react? It was almost as if he knew this was coming. She sat down on the front steps. Silence, empty silence, she was alone. After a few moments of staring at the front gate, she heard a helicopter above. The swirling deep sound seemed to snap her out of her trance. She had to do something, first things first, she will call his attorney. Then she will make a phone call to Mr.Jenkins, TJ's father. His parents needed to know what was happening. She didn't know how to explain this ridiculous mess. Even though Rum Mason is dead, he is still causing them pain.

"Hey, it's Reggie."

"Well hello Reggie, good to hear from you." Mr. Jenkins glanced over at his wife.

"I don't know where to start. Rum is dead. TJ has been arrested for murder." Her voice was shaking.

"They think TJ murdered Rum? Where is TJ? When did this happen?"

"TJ found Rum dead at his home several days ago. TJ was arrested today at our home less than an hour ago. I am not sure yet where they are taking him. I will let you know as soon as I know more."

"I must call our attorney and we can fly down as soon as possible." Mr. Jenkins was motioning for his wife to call their attorney.

"His attorney is aware and expected that he would hear from you. He told me to wait to hear from him before I do anything."

"We will call him now and let you know our plans." Mr. Jenkins was pacing back and forth.

After the phone calls were made. Reggie sat on her bed, not knowing what to do next. She knew TJ had the best attorneys around and all of this would be straightened out. It was just a matter of when he could come home. His attorney told her not to talk to anyone, with the exception of his parents. He said to wait until he gave her further information. She agreed.

She laid down on the bed with Sammy at her side. He purred loudly which helped her calm her nerves. She never dreamed of TJ being accused of murdering Rum. She will find out who murdered him. Her phone rang, she jumped up to answer.

"Sheriff Johnson, they took him. Why is TJ being accused of this? They got it wrong!"

"Reggie, the evidence or lack of, points at TJ. He was the one at the scene, no other fingerprints were found. No sign of anyone else being there. If he is innocent, he will be released." Sheriff Johnson wanted to reassure her but he was having a hard time with it too. Something wasn't right.

"If he is innocent? Of course he is innocent!" Reggie raised her voice in frustration.

She wasn't sure if the sheriff believed him or not. After the call ended, Reggie got down on her knees and prayed. She prayed the answers would come soon.

CHAPTER 28

Two days had passed since TJ's arrest. His attorney had flown to see him in Atlanta where TJ was being held. He filed for an expedited hearing. Reggie was packing to go stay in Atlanta and wait for the hearing to be held. She had only been able to talk with TJ a couple of times by phone. Two days had seemed like two weeks. This needed to be over with soon. She would stay in Atlanta for as long as needed. Their housekeeper would feed and take care of Sammy while she was gone.

TJ's parents were flying to meet her in Atlanta. Sheriff Johnson and his wife were going to meet her too. The luggage was in the back seat. She started up her car and sat in the driveway. She took several deep breaths, closing her eyes, breathing slowly in and out. She had her bag of gummy bears in the console but she really wanted a cigarette.

She arrived in Atlanta a few hours later, checked into the hotel waiting for the others to arrive. She laid on the bed waiting. Two hours had passed when she woke up suddenly because her cell phone was ringing.

"Reggie, we are still in Birch Creek. Domino showed up here at the sheriff's office and confessed to killing Rum!"

"What?" She sat up straight.

"Yes, he came in and confessed. I can't believe it either. We are holding him here for now.

TJ gets to go home." "When?"

"Apparently, his attorney is working on it right now. I am sure you will get a call soon." "I knew this would work out."

They ended the call. Reggie was getting the answer she needed.

Sheriff Johnson couldn't believe it when Domino came in to confess. The sheriff was called up to the front office and standing in the lobby was Domino. As soon as Domino spotted the sheriff, he raised up his hands.

"I'm here to surrender."

"Surrender?" Sheriff Johnson was cautious putting his hand on his gun holster. Domino took a step forward.

"I'm not armed. I want to make a confession. I murdered Rum Mason and kidnapped you." Domino had a determined look in his eye. Sheriff Johnson called for some back-up and asked the deputy to handcuff Domino. Let's walk back this way to the interview room. He asked the deputy to stay in the room with him while he called the FBI agent.

When the sheriff entered the room again, he asked Domino to write out a confession. The FBI will read and ask questions when they get here. He was instructed to write out two separate statements, one of the murder confession and one for the kidnapping confession.

Domino looked down at the paper with his identifying information at the top of each page. He hesitated briefly before speaking.

"My attorney is on his way and I don't want to write the statement until he arrives and is able to be present while I write it."

"When will the attorney be here?" Sheriff Johnson asked.

"Not sure, he is coming from Chicago."

"We have to detain you here until he arrives."

"I understand, he is aware of my intentions and should arrive soon." The sheriff left the deputy to stay with Domino while he went out to update the FBI and then called Reggie.

Reggie and TJ's parents met TJ at the FBI headquarters in Atlanta. Reggie ran to him as soon as he stepped into the office.

"Are you ok?" she looked at him..

"Yes" He hugged her and shook his attorney's hand. TJ hadn't realized his parents were until he turned back around. HIs mom reached out her arms.

"Mom and dad, thank you for coming, this means so much!"

"Of course." Mr. Jenkins replied.

The FBI agent motioned and said they were free to leave. A wave of relief flowed through Reggie as she took a deep breath and released it slowly.

"Thank God, let's get you home." TJ turned to his parents.

"Please come stay a few days with us since you are already here."

"Whatever you want." His mother responded.

Reggie noticed TJ was quiet on the way home and she didn't want to press him. She knew he probably hadn't slept in days and had been through an ordeal in jail in Atlanta. She was going to let him talk about it when he was ready. She just wanted to concentrate on the fact that he was now free.

Domino's attorney arrived within a couple of hours. He was no non-sense, straight to the point. He walked in the interview room, wearing his suit that was tailored exactly to his measurements. He asked to speak with his client alone. After 5 minutes, he said his client was ready to write his confession statement. The papers were given back to him with the prefilled heading. Domino took his time writing several pages of his confession. Once finished, his attorney read it over and handed the pages to the agent. His confession read:

Confidential Written Statement

Submitted by Domino Mendez

Location: Birch Creek Sheriff's office - Interview room

In the presence of: William Adams, Attorney; Special agent, Reed

Voluntary Statement - Domino Mendez:

I, Domino A. Mendez, am providing this statement voluntarily and of my own free will, with full understanding of my rights. I have not been coerced or threatened in any way. I am here to take responsibility for the actions I committed regarding the death of Rum Mason.

I knew Rum would come after me, since I disobeyed his directives. I wanted to find him first and catch him off-guard. I knew he could hide at his home in Birch Creek. I still had the key fob to enter the property. I entered the gate, parked my car just inside the gate and walked down the driveway to his house. He doesn't have cameras at the front gate. I still had my key to enter his home too. I knew he was home as soon as I stepped in. I could hear him in the kitchen. I made the decision to walk right in and confront him. He saw me and immediately pulled a gun on me. He taunted me saying no one could touch him, not the police, not Reggie, not anyone. Hostile words were exchanged. When he moved behind the counter, I knew what was about to happen. He had that look in his eye. I drew my gun and told him to stop. He lunged forward, I fired. He immediately fell, there was blood, I didn't check for a pulse. I wiped down all surfaces I had touched and grabbed his gun and left. Both firearms are in the Savannah River.

Voluntary Statement - Domino Mendez

I confess to the kidnapping of Sheriff Johnson under the direction and manipulation of Rum Mason. I was ordered to kidnap him by Rum. After kidnapping him, and a few days of captivity, I made the decision to let him go. I took him to Atlanta and let him go. After letting him go, I was threatened by 2 of Rum's associates that I had disobeyed orders and would pay for it. I knew that meant I was going to be killed.

Signed; Domino Mendez

Special Agent Reed, read him his rights and placed him under arrest. He was escorted out of the room to be placed in a holding cell and his attorney promptly left.

CHAPTER 29

Nick had been cleared of any wrongdoing; no charges were filed against him. Domino remained in jail, awaiting sentencing. And while the world seemed shocked by Domino's confession, Nick wasn't. Nick knew he and Domino were the next targets on Rum's list. Nick kept replaying his last phone with TJ. Had TJ figured out where Rum may have been hiding after that phone call? Had he tipped off Domino? The question lingered, unanswered. Despite everything, Nick genuinely wanted to help with Reggie and TJ's wedding, even if only behind the scenes. He hoped they knew he'd been cleared by the FBI. Still, part of him hesitated. Should he reach out or stay out of their way?

Nick was rebuilding his life among New York city's elite families and philanthropic circles. His event planning business was thriving again, invitations, fundraisers, exclusive galas were all back on his calendar. Betty had been such a good friend, confidant, and supported him emotionally through all of this. He had teamed up with her to use some of her flower arrangements and wreaths, tablecloths etc at some of these events. They were a success working together which helped him so much. Yet, despite the momentum, one thing still pulled at him: Reggie. He had promised her the wedding of her dreams, and part of him still wanted to make good on that promise. Not for recognition. Just to show her that some people did mean what they said.

That night after a successful charity event auction at a Fifth Avenue penthouse, Nick stepped outside on the balcony alone. He looked down at the city streets beneath, lights, traffic, people walking about everywhere, festive energy filled the air. But his thoughts were hundreds of miles away. He pulled out his phone hovering over Reggie's contact information, then began texting:

I know I should have reached out sooner, if you're willing to talk, I think you should know how Rum manipulated everyone, especially me.

He hesitated before hitting send, and just like that the past came rushing back. He needed to get this off his chest, he wanted to explain it to her.

Reggie stood at the kitchen counter, barefoot from coming in from the beach. Her glass of water half full was on the counter beside her phone. She was taking a sip when her phone buzzed. She picked it up and saw she had a text message. Nick. She froze, not really wanting to see what he had to say but curious too. She read his text.

"TJ, Nick just texted me." She called out so he could hear her out on the deck. "What does he want?" TJ 's jaw tightened.

"Apparently, he wants to talk. He says he was manipulated like everyone else by Rum." "Do you want to listen to what he has to say?"

"I don't know. Maybe." She laid her phone down, walking out onto the deck.

"I need to think about it. I feel like he was going to hurt us." She stared out at the surf for a few minutes. Then turning to TJ, she thought of when she saw him rolling his eyes when she saw Rum calling him before and telling her that he broke up with his partner.

"Do you think they broke up because he wasn't going to do what Rum wanted?"

"I'm thinking we should hear what he has to say, together. I will call him if you want me too." TJ pulled out his phone.

"No, not yet." Reggie wasn't ready to hear how Rum planned to hurt them. She didn't want to respond to his text either. She would sleep on it and see if she felt different tomorrow.

The next morning she woke up to the smell of coffee. The sun was up, Sammy was still sleeping at the foot of the bed. TJ was drinking his coffee out on the deck when she walked into the kitchen. She smelled TJ's spinach quiche cooking in the oven. It was her favorite meal he cooks. She walked out on the deck, leaned down to kiss TJ when he pulled her onto his lap, kissing and hugging her.

"Good morning, Gorgeous!"

"Good morning to you, handsome. I love you." "Have you made a decision yet about calling Nick?" "Yes, let's call him after we eat that amazing quiche."

TJ's parents were not up yet. He cooked an extra one for them to be ready when they got up. After breakfast, Reggie went out on the deck with TJ. They sat down and called Nick.

The phone rang twice before Nick picked up. "Reggie?"

His voice was quiet, tentative. He was nervous about what she had to say.

"I wasn't sure if I should call." She said as she was staring out at the ocean. The breeze felt cool and crisp.

"I've thought about what you wrote in your text. I know Rum was an evil person so I want to hear your side of things."

"Thank you for calling and giving me a chance to talk about it. I wanted to reach out sooner but every time I started, I wasn't sure where to begin."

"How about the truth?" She said softly.

Nick paused to gather his thoughts.

"I didn't know how deep Rum's manipulation went," Nick said finally. Silence - then Nick began again.

"At first, he was charming and generous. He acted like he wanted my business. He made promises, got me clients, I thought he was just well-connected. But he was weaving me into something darker. Quietly."

Reggie closed her eyes, knowing it was the truth. "He always had an angle."

"He used me. I wasn't exactly sure what all his business dealings were about and I didn't pry nor did I want to know. Whenever someone crossed him or challenged him, he had a vendetta against them. I wanted to walk away, but he reminded me of the favors he had done for me, the debts I didn't realize I owed. I felt trapped."

"Did you know what he was planning?" She asked.

"Some of it but not everything, but I knew the pressure was building. I knew you and TJ were next. And I knew if I stayed quiet, I was helping him." Nick took a deep breath, slowly exhaling.

"Is that why you broke up?"

"Yes, He wanted me to hurt you and others and I couldn't do it, I didn't want to do it. I realized how brainwashed I was, I just wanted to cut him out of my life. He didn't care about me, he only cared about himself. Cared about himself."

Reggie didn't speak for a moment. Then:

"I don't really want to know what he wanted you to do. You hurt me, I trusted you to plan the most important day of my life. You hurt me, Nick. But I believe you."

Nick leaned back in his chair, a rush of relief washed over him. "Thank you, Reggie."

"This has been a nightmare with many people hurt, even killed and so many lives ruined.

Families still have missing daughters, sisters, cousins, relatives. You were a part of the damage, maybe not directly but you had to know some of it." Reggie's speech became stronger as she spoke those words. It felt good to express her thoughts.

"Reggie, I want to help put all of this to rest and help as much as I can to find those who are missing. I have already written down everything I can remember that I think could help the FBI. I started making notes weeks ago as thoughts entered my mind."

"Alright, then let's start there." Reggie said. TJ nodded his head agreeing with Reggie's statement.

"Ok, I'm not sure exactly what you mean but I'm ready."

They talked for a few minutes, planning to meet in a couple of days in New York. After she hung up the call, TJ reached over to hug her.

"It's all going to be fine now." He said hugging her tight. TJ's parents were in the kitchen pouring their coffee when TJ came in from the deck. He pulled the quiche from the oven serving their plates to them. He joined them at the table.

"I am curious about something your attorney said to me." his father said, picking up his fork to take a bite.

"What is it?"

"He said one of his colleagues was in Georgia too. His colleague was representing Domino, the one who murdered Rum. It's ironic isn't it that 2 attorney's from the same firm are both here in Georgia representing you and Domino both connected to Rum?"

"Well, we both have good representation then. It's a good law firm." He smiled at his father. "Very coincidental." His father said as he took a bite.

"Yes, it is. Need more coffee?" TJ asked.

Reggie sat curled on the edge of the couch, a blanket draped over her legs, Sammy laid on top of her legs. TJ walked in watching her. He knew she was in deep thought but she looked so peaceful. She looked up, catching him staring at her.

"What do you think about asking Nick to finish planning our wedding?" She asked. He raised an eyebrow.

"You want to let him back in?"

"I think we should," she said quietly. "Not because we owe him anything, but because maybe this is how we close the circle."

"Do you trust him?" He leaned back.

"I trust that he wants to make this right."

TJ looked at her for a long moment. Then he gave a slow nod. "Alright, let's re-hire him for our wedding planner."

She smiled, relieved.

"I'll ask him in New York."

CHAPTER 30

The cafe in Soho was tucked between a florist and a bookstore, it was private where they could meet and talk about Nick's notes. Reggie had arrived early, wanting to get a table away from the crowd. She also loved watching the New Yorkers. She was used to the small town diner in Birch Creek where the locals came to eat and were never in a hurry.

She noticed how the customers at this cafe' seemed to be in a hurry, no friendly conversations about the weather, the crops or the sick family member. Nick arrived on time.

"Thanks for coming," Nick sat down across from her. "I'm glad you reached out."

They ordered coffee and were silent for a moment. Reggie studied him, he looked polished as usual but tired like a weight on his shoulders.

"How are you doing living here in New York?"

"It's just what I needed. I love it, business is picking up. Do you want to order anything to eat? Their bagels are delicious."

"Pie would be good." Reggie said as she looked at the menu. They ordered pie and bagels.

Then Reggie got down to business.

"Nick, I want to ask you something before we dive into your notes." Nick raised his eyebrow. "Ok."

"We want you back as our wedding planner, are you interested?" He blinked. "Seriously?"

"You know us and what kind of wedding I dreamed of and really after everything....there's a strange kind of peace knowing you are a part of it."

Nick let out a slow breath, clearly moved. "Yes, of course, I won't let you down." "I know you won't." She smiled.

"Reggie, I have a wonderful friend, Betty, who I work with often now. She has helped and supported me through all of this. She does some amazing floral arrangements that I would like for you to look at. If you approve, I would like to ask her to help me."

"Yes, of course. Go ahead and tell her to work with you on the flowers for the wedding and the reception."

"Thank you, that means so much to me." Nick looked away for a brief moment.

"Now let's look at your notes." Reggie was curious as to what he had written.

Nick pulled out a small black notebook from his coat pocket.

"I started writing things down, some of it makes no sense but it may mean something to the FBI. I have written locations Rum mentioned and places we lived and visited, names I have heard him say and people he talked to on the phone and his patterns."

"Patterns?" Reggie asked.

"Yes, how he purchased new cell phones each month, how he moved money, and how he gave direct orders almost in codes."

Reggie opened the notebook gently, flipping through the pages. Each entry was neatly written with questions added and circles and arrows drawn, like he was mind-mapping his past. It was his past memories that now haunt him.

"Nick, this notebook along with more interviews with you could really help find the other missing people."

Nick looked away again for a moment trying to collect his thoughts.

"Reggie, I really want to help, I want to make this right."

"I'm going to help you make it right." She nodded while drinking a sip of coffee.

"I really don't know if any of this will help, it's just certain things and names that I started remembering once I had a chance to think about it. I can answer any questions the FBI might have after they look at these notes. I hope the FBI can find some of these people that I have listed here. They may be willing to talk too.

CHAPTER 31

Reggie slid into a booth across from Special agent Reed. She had rushed over in the rain to meet him. She pulled out the sealed envelope with the notebook inside from her bag.

"I think these notes could be very useful."

"Is this what you mentioned on the call?" He asked before breaking open the seal.

Reggie nodded.

"It's everything Nick remembers - names, places, comments he remembers, patterns of his banking and cell phone tactics."

The agent opened the envelope sliding out the notebook. He started reading the first couple of pages.

"If this gives us movement, we will owe you both," he said as he closed the notebook, putting it back in the envelope.

"Nick said he is willing to answer any questions you may have to the best of his recollection." The agent stood.

"You trust Nick?" he asked.

"Yes, he wants to help." Her words were confident.

"I'll be in touch." he said as he walked away.

Reggie sat sipping her coffee, watching the people flow in and out. The smell of the coffee shop reminded her of Darlene's restaurant back home. Damn, she missed those pies. She laughed to herself thinking about how she would eat pie for breakfast and then go outside and smoke a cigarette. A cigarette, she thought, the smell of the lit end and the taste of it being inhaled, that sounded good right now.

CHAPTER 32

Domino sat at the table in his orange jumpsuit.

"No handcuffs needed." Agent Reed motioned for the deputy to take off the handcuffs.

Domino nodded thanking the agent for the gesture.

"You said you are willing to help us beyond your current case. So, let's talk."

"Yes, I want to help clean up the mess Rum left behind. I will give you what I can."

"Were you security or a transporter for Rum?" The agent was making notes.

"I was whatever Rum needed me to be. I did security and transportation."

"We are working on some of the investigations that are tied to Rum here in the United States in Charleston, Savannah and Macon. Did you travel all around or stay in one area?"

Domino laughed.

"I was one of the ones who traveled all around, wherever Rum told me to go. Rum kept it all layered, many levels. There were a few who knew more than they let on."

"Like who?" He leaned in to hear the names.

"You need to talk to Slim. His name is Miguel. I'm trying to remember his last name. I know he is one of the team that got arrested and sent to prison."

"You think he has information that he will share?" He was writing down his name.

"He doesn't have anything to lose now. I think it's Alvarez, yeah, that sounds right." He knows tech inside and out, he is the drone guy. He knows all about drone surveillance and sabotage."

"Sabotage?"

"Yes, and more. He bragged about doing silent strikes that never hit the news media." "So, why do you want to give us all of this now? You want a reduced sentence?'

Domino leaned forward.

"Because I was part of the chain. I can't fix what I did and I know I have to pay for it but I can help break it before someone else ends up gone. Others will try to mimic Rum."

Silence filled the room as Special Agent Reed made his notes.

"You think missing girls are still out there that can be found alive?"

"Yes. Look for an abandoned warehouse off HWY 17. They used it like a weigh station. They only kept them there for short periods but some could still be there."

"We are going to have to verify all of this."

"Do it, talk to Slim. You will understand how deep all of this goes after talking to him." He sat back. "Rum was dirty and stayed clean on the outside. Some of his team may not even know he is dead yet. You will discover a lot of people involved in this who definitely don't want it to go public."

"Thank you for all of this, I will be back in touch." Agent Reed signaled for the guard.

CHAPTER 33

TJ stepped into a high-rise law office, far from the buzz of Michigan Avenue. He nodded as he walked past the receptionist. She didn't ask questions, smiled and nodded back. She led him into a private conference room, where the attorney, Mr. Adams, was already waiting. He stood and shook TJ's hand. The rain was streaming down the large windows steadily on this windy, rainy Chicago day.

"He's holding up," the attorney said, sitting back down. "You've got everything you need?"

"I've got statements, psychological background, parole probabilities, character angles. If the prosecution pushes for more than five years, I'll crush them." TJ's jaw tightened.

"No loose ends? Make sure he is taken care of." "He will be."

"What about the media coverage, what are they saying?"

The attorney scrolled down his tablet looking for the latest news story.

"Most outlets are echoing the press release. They talk about self-defense, prior threat, Rum's history and a couple mention that you found the body." He looked up.

"I want my name left out of it. We don't need anymore news coverage."

"Law enforcement corroborated the facts given of the scene. There is no physical evidence to contradict him."

"Alright then." TJ nodded and left the room.

CHAPTER 34

Slim sat back in his metal chair like he owned the room. Across from him were 2 special agents, Reed and Jones. Slim's tattoos covered most of the skin on his slim body.

"We are recording this interview today with Miguel "Slim"Alvarez." Jones spoke into the recorder. Agent Reed began talking:

"We are investigating operations linked to Rumsfeld Mason. We have been told that you ran surveillance for him?" He posed it as a statement and question.

"I see Domino's been talkin'."

"This isn't about Domino. We are here to find out more about Rum's operations and an alleged drone strike that hit a home in Birch Creek last year. We are asking if you were involved?"

"You're asking if I flew the bird that lit up that cop's house?" Slim was grinning. He shrugged and leaned forward.

"Yeah, it was me."

"I need you to confirm for the record that you operated the drone that set fire to the residence of Detective Regina Memphis in Birch Creek?"

Slim nodded.

"I pulled the trigger myself, Rum's orders."

"You are saying that Rumsfeld Mason ordered a drone strike on Detective Regina Memphis's home?"

"Yes, he said she was poking her nose too far into his deals. He said make it burn. So I did.

I used one of Chinatech's private prototypes. Q8 series, built with thermal targeting." "Ok, that confirms that he ordered the strike." Reed looked over at Jones

CHAPTER 35

The agents sat around a table cluttered with folders, photos, and a single tablet replaying the recording of Slim's interview.

"I pulled the trigger myself, Rum's orders." Jones clicked off the recording.

"That's the link, we have Rum tied to the drone strike on Detective Memphis's house." The supervisor nodded.

"Is Chinatech still running without Rum?" Reed asked.

"Doubtful, but get it checked out." The supervisor directed. They continued looking over their notes of both interviews and Nick's notebook trying to piece together some of the timelines and places they lived. They were each assigned some of the names listed in the notebook.

They were ordered to find them, interview them and see what else they knew about Rum and his network.

"Sir, if they aren't already in prison, then we won't get too much out of them. If they are connected to Rum's network, they will be afraid to talk even if he is dead. They will be fearful of going to jail."

"Start with the ones in jail first. Figure it out." The supervisor walked out of the room.

CHAPTER 36

TJ and Reggie were back home in St. Simons, happy, content and looking forward to their future. Nick had traveled to Georgia this time to meet with Reggie again. They were meeting at a coffee shop in the downtown area of St. Simon's near the fishing pier.

The coffee shop was quiet, it was early morning. Reggie sat across from Nick, reviewing his plans for the decorations for the wedding reception at the pavilion.

"These look perfect." Reggie said smiling. She took a sip of her coffee. "Now show me the maps you talked about."

Nick pulled out printouts and maps based on the notes that Reggie turned over to the FBI. Reggie sipped her coffee, eyes focused on a highlighted section.

"You really wrote all of this from memory" Nick nodded.

"Yeah, some of it came back at night in dreams or random flashbacks. It wasn't just what Rum said to me or what I overheard him saying, it was what other people have said about him too. I was trying to think back on everything, running it over and over in my head. When TJ called me one night, I realized I could really help by remembering random experiences and trying to think like Rum."

Reggie's hand froze mid-page. Nick didn't notice and kept talking.

"I said that Rum doesn't forgive or forget, he resets and that he probably was hiding in plain sight."

Reggie looked up.

"Wait, when did TJ call you?"

"It was late one night, I figured you were with him. I don't know, a couple of days before Rum was murdered. Why?"

"TJ never told me he called you." Nick's eyebrows lifted.

"Really, I just assumed you both were checking leads."

Reggie said nothing for a moment. Her stomach turned, not from what Nick said but from what TJ hadn't said.

Nick continued.

"He seemed determined to find him. He loves you so much and I could tell he was worried about what Rum might be planning."

Reggie felt tightening in her chest. She smiled at Nick. "Thanks for telling me."

Nick looked confused but nodded. "Of course."

CHAPTER 37

Sheriff Johnson sat across from Domino, separated by the plexiglass partition. Staring at first, then Sheriff Johnson spoke.

"I wanted to talk with you about why you came to my office to turn yourself in and confessed.

Why?"

"Because another man was being accused of a crime and he was innocent." Domino said remaining very calm.

"Are you wanting to be a hero now?" Sheriff Johnson leaned forward. "I don't care about being anybody's hero."

"So, since you couldn't let your conscience bother you about someone else being accused of murder, why did you kidnap me? Your conscience didn't bother you then?"

Domino sat up straight, clenched his jaw.

"Rum gave an order. I had to follow his orders. He wanted someone who was close to Reggie to be taken. You were the chosen one."

"Did you choose me or did Rum.?" The sheriff was frowning.

"I chose you. I knew you would survive it. Rum never got back to me and I didn't have a reason to keep holding you hostage, so I let you go."

"Did Rum know it was me you kidnapped?"

"Yes, following orders all this time is what kept me alive. The day I let you go was the day I stopped and I was going to be killed."

The sheriff stood up, grabbed his hat. He left without saying another word.

CHAPTER 38

The courtroom buzzed with hushed voices as people gathered into the gallery. A few reporters sat near the back, legal pads open, already taking notes. Domino sat at the defense table in a gray suit, polished, and calm. His attorney stood at this side, confident and in control.

TJ and Reggie sat quietly behind the bar, second row. They sat quietly taking it all in. The judge entered, everyone stood.

"Court is now is session in the matter of The State of Georgia vs Domino Mendez, case # 2124-A. Charges: Second degree homicide and unlawful restraint."

Once everyone was seated, Domino's attorney stood.

"We are not contesting that my client fired the weapon that ended Rumsfeld Mason's life. But the circumstances surrounding that event are critical here. This was not a cold blooded killing. This was survival, self-defense." He turned facing and pointed at Domino.

"My client feared for his life. Mr. Mason was armed. He had a history of violence. The prosecution will attempt to dismiss Mr. Mason's history and lifestyle but we will bring it all into perspective." He returned to his seat.

TJ and Reggie sat watching the attorney's, the jury, Domino and the judge. Judge Wells was apparently known for his conservative views and interpretation of the law. He was fair, slow to make rulings but thorough.

The prosecution began calling witnesses: forensic experts, local law enforcement. The testimony was very dry, clinical.

Then came Reggie.

She stepped onto the stand, wearing a navy dress, looking polished and sophisticated. She was nervous but confident. She answered the prosecutor's questions about Rum's history, his threats, the people he hurt.

"Did you consider Mr. Mason dangerous?"

"Hell, yes." She wanted to stress that answer. "Absolutely."

"Do you know this man sitting here on trial, Mr. Domino Mendez?" "No, I don't." She said.

"That's all I have your honor." The prosecutor sat down. That's all he has?, Reggie thought to herself.

Domino's attorney rose for cross examination.

"So, you don't know Mr. Domino Mendez, but you knew Mr. Mason?" "That is correct." She adjusted her sitting position.

"How did you know Mr. Mason?"

"I knew him due to an investigation that I worked on when 3 girls from Birch Creek went missing which turned into an international FBI investigation due to Mr. Mason running the largest human trafficking ring in the world." She blurted out.

The Prosecutor stood.

"I object, Mr. Mason was never charged with any crimes."

Before the judge had a chance to speak, Reggie blurted out, "That's because he is now dead, he would have been charged."

The judge hit the gavel.

"Sustained, I won't have any outbursts, Ms. Memphis."

"That's all I have for this witness, your honor." Domino's attorney turned toward Reggie. "You can step down now, Ms. Memphis."

TJ was smiling, he knew Reggie was determined to get her point across about Rum Mason. TJ winked at her when she sat down next to him.

"All rise, we will now break for lunch." The bailiff said.

Once outside of the courtroom, Reggie thought about her testimony.

"He asked if I knew Domino, I know he is going to paint a picture of us not knowing Domino and how do we know or not know what he is capable of. I don't know what he is capable of but I do know what Rum was capable of!"

Tj took her hand.

"It's all going to be ok. This trial is about Domino, not Rum. Domino did some very bad things but I am sure his story is correct, it was self-defense."

After lunch, everyone gathered back into the courtroom. The prosecutor stood. "Now the state calls Mr. Domino Mendez to the stand."

The courtroom was quiet with only the tapping of the prosecutor's pen. Domino sat at the stand, calm, jaw tight. The Prosecutor got up, walked over to the stand and leaned in close to Domino, just trying to unsettle him.

"Mr. Mendez, you said previously that you entered Rum Mason's home around 7:45PM, is that correct?"

"That's right."

"And that you were there alone, correct?" "Yes," Domino's jaw tightened.

"No one else was there when you fired the weapon?" "No."

The prosecutor paused, glancing at the jury as he walked over to the evidence table. He picked up a paper.

"How did you enter Mr. Mason's house?" The prosecutor looked over at the jury again. "I entered through the front door, I had a key." Domino shifted in his seat.

"I would like for you to look at this printout, it's a record of when the doors opened at Rum's house. Tell me about the back door opening, what does the printout say?"

"It says that the back door to the patio opened at 7:15." "That is a full 30 minutes before you said you arrived."

"Ok, I'm not following what you're getting at." Domino said. "Was someone else there before you arrived?"

"Hell if I know. No one else except Rum was there when I arrived. Rum could have gone out the back door."

"So, you admit to trespassing with a loaded weapon?" Domino's attorney objected but the judge allowed the question.

"I didn't go there to shoot him. I wanted to find him and turn him in. But when he came at me...he looked down, I had to defend myself."

"What did you do with your weapon?" he asked.

"I threw it in the Savannah River." "What did you do with Rum's gun?" "I threw it in the Savannah River."

"So, we have no way of knowing if Rum even had a gun do we? No further questions, your honor."

It was now time for Domino's attorney to question him and set the story straight. "Mr. Mendez, you didn't go to Rum's house to commit murder did you?"

"No, never."

"You went there because...?"

"Because I was scared. I knew what Rum had done to people. What he could still do. I needed to find him and turn him in."

"What could he still do to people like Nick, His former lover; like Reggie Memphis and TJ Jenkins, like yourself and like all the girls still missing?"

"He was never going to stop, and I didn't want a part of that anymore." "And you brought a weapon because..?"

"I didn't trust him. I thought if I showed up armed, he'd back down. But when he came at me, fast and aggressive, I panicked. It was instinct and self-defense."

"You thought your life was in danger?" "Yes."

"Why did you throw both guns in the Savannah River?"

"Well, I was not planning to be caught. I didn't plan to turn myself in until I saw an innocent man being arrested for a crime he didn't commit. I couldn't have lived with that."

"No further questions, your honor."

CHAPTER 39

It was late afternoon, the jurors were settling in the room to deliberate. Twelve jurors will decide the guilt or innocence of a man who already confessed to killing Rum Mason. The question to be answered was self defense or murder? The aroma of fresh coffee filled the room as the door shut behind them. Each juror looked at their notes before beginning to speak. The clock on the wall ticked loudly with the silence taking over the room. Juror #4 looked up at the clock.

"Are we ready to take a vote?" she asked. Female, early 60's. "I've got questions." Juror #9 said. Male, mid-30's.

Chairs scooted back as others looked around the room.

Juror #1, the forman, male 40ish stood up.

"Alright, Let's talk about it. What questions do you have?" he asked.

"No murder weapon, not one. Not even shell casings recovered. Just a body, a confession, and a timeline that no one seems to be able to verify?"

Juror #7 - female, 40's:

"He turned himself in, that counts for something."

Juror #9:

"Maybe. Or maybe he knew the walls were closing in and this was the only way he could control the story."

Juror #3 (elderly man):

"The sheriff said Rum had a temper. Domino's story makes sense. Rum came at him and he reacted. If someone lunged at me in that kitchen....

Juror #11:

"Except no one can say what happened, we only have his version."

Juror #9:

"And what about Terrence "TJ" Jenkins, he is the one who found the body. Why didn't he testify?"

Juror #1:

"Hmmm, that is a good point." Silence in the room again for a moment.

Juror #12 (quiet woman):

"The attorney pulled him from the witness list. Maybe he didn't want to complicate the case?" She spoke softly.

Juror #7:

"Maybe there's something he couldn't explain." Silence filled the room again.

Juror #4:

"More coffee anyone?"

Juror #1:

"Let's focus on the facts, no assumptions. Domino said he threw the guns in the Savannah River so they couldn't be found. He wasn't planning to ever get caught until he saw that TJ was being arrested for murder."

Juror #9:

"All of sudden he had a moral compass?"

Juror # 4:

"Maybe, but we are just supposed to take his word for it?"

Juror #3:

"It could be the truth."

Juror #1:

"Alright, let's take a preliminary vote to see where we stand. We can dig deeper." He stood and grabbed the marker for the white board. He wrote a big "G" and then a big "NG" on the board. He pointed at each juror to give their vote. He marked both sides of the board. They would dig deeper.

CHAPTER 40

Time seemed to stand still as the clock ticked louder than usual. Reggie and TJ sat on the worn leather sofa in Sheriff Johnson's office while waiting on a verdict. Sheriff Johnson sipped his strong, stale coffee, fingers tapping on the desk. His phone rang and they jumped.

"Sheriff Johnson" He answered.

He paused and shifted in his chair. He looked over at Reggie.

"She is actually here in my office right now."

Reggie looked surprised and glanced at TJ. The sheriff frowned as he listened to the words on the other end of the call. When he hung up, he turned to Reggie.

"That was Special Agent Reed."

"What is it?" She stood up sensing something was wrong.

"They confirmed it was Rum who ordered the drone strike on your house. One of his men confessed. The drone was a private prototype from Chinatech."

TJ stood.

"Well, we already knew it was him, this just confirms it. He's dead, nothing can be done now." TJ sat back down.

"What else was that man capable of doing? I can't even imagine." She said, "Let's go back to the courthouse and wait on the verdict." She turned to TJ.

"That could be hours from now, how about we go see Darlene and eat some of that good pie?"

"Yes, I like that idea. C'mon Sheriff and go with us." Reggie smiled.

CHAPTER 41

The courtroom was packed. They had received word that the jury had reached a verdict.

Sheriff Johnson stood in the back, arms crossed, stone faced. Reggie and TJ sat in the gallery again, same seats as before. Domino sat at the defense table. He looked straight ahead. The bailiff stood as the jury entered the courtroom.

"All rise."

The room was silent as the foreperson stood and handed the slip of paper to the clerk, who passed it to the judge. Everyone waited with anticipation, eyes fixed on the judge.

"In the matter of the state vs Domino Alejandro Mendez..." The judge paused.

"On the charge of unlawful restraint of Sheriff Johnson: this court finds the defendant guilty.

On the charge of second degree homicide in the death of Rumsfeld Mason, by reason of self-defense and the presence of mitigating factors, this court finds the defendant not guilty."

Domino exhaled sharply, lowering his head. He didn't celebrate. He didn't even look relieved, just tired. His attorney leaned in, whispering something to him. Domino nodded.

The judge continued. "The defendant will remain in custody pending sentencing on the remaining conviction. The court is adjourned."

The gavel hit the block. Reggie noticed TJ had no reaction to any of the verdicts, he was just unreadable. Reggie knew Domino was guilty of kidnapping Sheriff Johnson, obviously, but didn't think he deserved to be charged with murder of Rum. She was happy the verdict turned out how it did. Domino will serve his time for what he did.

"What do you think, TJ?" she asked.

"I think the jury got it right." no expression on his face.

CHAPTER 42

The sun was peeking through the trees shining on the very spot where her garden used to be. Reggie looked at the landscape where her house once stood. TJ stayed back at the car giving her a moment to reflect. The grass had grown back and small pines had started growing. Reggie glanced down the driveway remembering the day Freddie parked his truck at the foot of the driveway, her pleading with him not to do it. That seemed like a lifetime ago now. She stood still.

"I tried to save you, Freddie. I really did." She said softly to herself.

The wind started blowing, giving her a cool chill. She thought of Kendra, Myra and Natalie, and the other girls who were saved. Others didn't make it or haven't been found yet but she didn't want to give up hope for them. They will be found, the FBI is closing in now. She knew it was time for her to build her new life. TJ walked up putting his arm around her.

"My house burned, but I didn't." It's time to move forward." She looked one last time where the house stood and then turned towards the car. No going back.

"Reggie, You like living in St. Simons, right?"

"I love living in St. Simons. Growing up here taught me a lot but that chapter is over with now and I don't regret any of it. I'm ready to move forward, TJ."

"No regrets!"

CHAPTER 43

The TV over the counter was tuned to a national morning news show. A red breaking news banner ran across the bottom. Customers looked up and the room went silent as they listened. The barista stopped.

"We're following breaking developments this morning in a high-profile federal investigation that began in Georgia and now stretches all the way to Washington DC and beyond.

Multiple young women have been recovered in coordinated overnight raids in South Carolina and Virginia. This comes after the recent trial of a former employee linked to the late Rumsfeld Mason's private network.

What began as a local missing persons investigation has now uncovered ties to a larger human trafficking operation that federal sources confirm may implicate multiple public figures."

The footage showed a gated estate in Northern Virginia. Then to a shot of a blurred-out man being loaded into a black SUV, handcuffs on barely visible under his coat.

"Sources tell us one of the men arrested served as a senior advisor to a member of congress. No official charges have been announced yet, but more names are expected."

TJ stood at the counter, watching. Reggie entered just as the news anchor continued with the story:

"The girls rescued last night range in age from fourteen to nineteen. Authorities say the operation was made possible in part by information provided by a confidential informant already in custody. Investigators are now examining how much of Rum's influence reached into public contracts, foreign manufacturing deals, and high-ranking security circles."

TJ glanced at Reggie, her eyes focused on the screen. The story ended and was cut to commercial.

"It's not over, more will come out." Reggie said as she walked to the table.

"No, but this time we are staying clear of it all." TJ looked at her waiting for some assurance.

CHAPTER 44

Nick smiled at the camera lights as flashes blinded him momentarily. The press had been invited for a brief segment as this was a big fundraiser for the women's shelter in New York City. A reporter stepped up just as he was posing with a donor.

"Mr. Nick Daniels, can you comment on your association with Rumsfeld Mason's human trafficking network? It is ironic that you are here for a fundraiser for a women's shelter." Nick stopped smiling, he felt his stomach turn. The camera's caught his expression.

"I was hired as a planner," he said nervously.

Another reporter spoke up:

"Were you aware that girls were being trafficked at events that you organized?" The crowd got quiet. The music turned down. Nick put down his champagne flute.

"No, I didn't know what he was involved in."

"You were with Rum Mason as his lover for years, you are saying you didn't know any of it.?"

"No, I didn't," he repeated.

Nick needed to vomit. He excused himself to go to the bathroom. He needed to get out of there. He leaned against the bathroom wall. Breathing slowly in and out. He had to find a way to walk out of this event, his career would be ruined. He heard a knock and a familiar voice at the door. It was Betty.

"Nick, let me in. I'm going to walk with you out the door and take you home." He opened the door.

"Thank you, Betty. I wasn't ready for reporters to question me." He hugged her.

"I know, let's walk out with our heads held high. I won't let them get to you. You are going to be fine. I will help you write a statement as a press release. We will get it all straightened out." She held his hand and pulled him out of the bathroom.

CHAPTER 45

The next morning as the sheriff passed the parking lot of the Sheriff's office, he saw media vans out front. He pulled into the back parking lot to avoid the reporters. As he walked in the back door, Ed greeted him.

"Good morning, Sheriff Johnson. Those reporters are here asking questions about the drone strike and wanting other information about Rum's network. I think you should answer a question or two and then make them leave."

"Yes, let's get this over with." He put on his hat and proceeded out the front door.

"Sheriff Johnson, What is your reaction to the drone strike being linked to Rumsfeld Mason?" They all crowded around him waiting on his response.

"I'm glad the truth came out. Wish it had come sooner."

"Can you tell us about your kidnapping ordeal? Did you know Rum had ordered it."

Sheriff Johnson didn't want to speak of his kidnapping, it was over and done and a memory that keeps him up at night.

"That's old news. No more questions. I need you all to move on so we can carry out our law enforcement duties. Thank you all for coming." He smiled and walked back inside.

Ed followed him to his office.

"You handled that well, sheriff."

"Sit down. I have something to tell you." The sheriff sat down in his office chair. Ed sat on the leather sofa.

"Ed, I have decided that it is time for me to retire. I'm going to retire in a couple of months and I'm going to suggest that you take my place." He smiled at Ed.

"Sir, I am flattered that you think I can do the job but I am not ready for that. Are you sure about retirement?" Ed's face flushed.

"More than sure. You need to get ready to take over. You will be interim until the next election, then I expect you to run a winning campaign."

"Have you told Reggie yet?"

"No, I will tell her at the wedding reception."

CHAPTER 46

Kendra clocked out at the flooring company at 5:00pm. She was walking to the parking lot with her coworker when a reporter with a camera man approached her:

"Tell us about your recollection of being kidnapped? How has it affected you?"

Her coworker stepped aside but stayed close, ready to protect Kendra. Kendra was startled with being approached and wondering how they knew it was her.

"I have no comment at this time. I will be holding a press conference in a couple of weeks with my team from "Her Voice.""

"Can you tell us more about "Her Voice?" the reporter leaned in.

"Her Voice is an organization I started to help victims of human trafficking. We want to educate communities and bring awareness to the fact that it happens everywhere even in your own small town. You will hear stories of what these victims went through and how you can help. It will be held at Birch Creek High school, please come." Kendra started walking away with her coworker.

"What do you think about Domino killing Rum?" the reporter shouted.

"No comment." Kendra reached her car door, waving bye to her coworker. She sat in her car waiting for the news van to leave the parking lot. She didn't want to be followed. As she sat in her car thinking about just being approached, she started crying. She cried not out of fear but because she was so happy she could now speak up with confidence. She has been able to heal while helping others learn to speak up. She was going to hold a press conference and then a town hall meeting at the local high school. These women will be empowered to continue telling their story and educating others. She was going to be reunited with Myra and Natalie too, the other hometown girls who went missing. She wiped her tears, started the car and drove home.

CHAPTER 47

The old chapel in Birch Creek looked like something on a painting or postcard.

Whitewashed wood, wild flowers trailing the fence line, and the sunlight peeking through the dense trees by the river. It looked as though a spotlight was pointing straight at the front steps. There were no reporters, no tension, just peace.

Inside the small country chapel, the pews were filled with family and friends all excited for Reggie and TJ on their wedding day. Nick had made the chapel look elegant yet simple, it was perfect. Sheriff Johnson was wearing a black tuxedo as he walked up to Reggie getting out of the limousine.

"Reggie, you look so beautiful."

Reggie's wedding dress was a sleeveless elegant silk gown with lace at the waist. She was wearing cowboy boots that looked perfect for this wedding scene.

"You clean up really nice yourself, sheriff." She was smiling nervously.

"Are you ready?" He asked.

Reggie took a deep breath and let it out slowly.

"Yes, I can't believe this day is finally here."

"Savor this moment, take it all in." Sheriff Johnson whispered. He held his arm up for Reggie to put her arm through his. They slowly walked up the front steps and waited. The front doors were shut so the guests and more importantly TJ couldn't see her yet. Nick was waiting outside on the steps ready to open the doors when the music began to play. Nick kissed her cheek and told her how amazing she looked. The music began. Nick opened the doors, Sheriff Johnson and Reggie slowly walked arm in arm. The guests were standing and TJ was standing there front and center with Ed who was officiating the ceremony. Reggie laughed when she saw TJ wearing her cowboy hat. She had never seen him in a cowboy hat. He was smiling with tears in his eyes when they arrived at the altar.

"Nice touch," Reggie said as looked up at the hat on his head.

"I wanted to fit in, " he said. Then he took the hat off and handed it to the sheriff.

Their vows described their love for each other, very sweet, not lengthy, not grand.

After the ceremony, the guests followed the path to the newly built pavilion down by the river. The pavilion stood tall with the big beams and rock pathways and patios. The art monuments were installed along the winding paths. String lights were glowing in the trees. Wildflowers were in bloom everywhere. Near the entrance to the pavilion stood a bronze plaque already installed.

Purple Mountains Majesty Park

Gifted to the people of Birch Creek by Mr. and Mrs. Terrence J. Jenkins

In honor of healing, hope, and home

There were walking paths leading to the tree line by the river and to the spot where the purple mountains were seen every evening. A small wooden stage stood at the bottom of the amphitheater just waiting for musicians in the future to become discovered. It was a perfect park for the Birch Creek community.

Lanterns swayed overhead, the guitar music was perfect. The guests were seated at the long farm tables with plates filled with delicious food from Chicago. A big table on the side was filled with lots of Darlene's pies. Reggie could see Darlene smiling as the guests commented on the tasty pies as she and TJ danced slowly to the rhythm of the guitar. When the music stopped, they made their way over to the table where they were to be seated with TJ's family, sheriff Johnson, his wife and Ed. After several toasts were made, Sheriff Johnson leaned over to Reggie.

"Well, you did it girl! I couldn't be any happier for you."

"Thank you for being a part of this special day. It means alot." She patted his hand.

He looked around at the pavilion and took a deep breath.

"This is going to be a great place for the families of Birch Creek."

"TJ wanted to give something back. I think he loves it here just as much as I do."

"There is something I want to tell you before the word gets out." He paused. "I'm retiring in a couple of months." He stared at her, not sure how she would react.

"Congratulations, I am happy for you. I think that is a wise decision."

"Ed will take my place as interim sheriff until the elections."

"He is the best choice to take your place. I will contribute very generously to his campaign.

Tell me he will run."

"If you and I have anything to do with it, he won't have a choice." They laughed and hugged each other.

Later in the evening as the reception was winding down, Reggie noticed the steeple on the chapel through the trees. She had found her prince and married him in the chapel that gave her such solace as a child. She looked at the steeple then back at TJ, she had never seen him look more handsome than he did in that moment. They had made it. She was finally Mrs. Terrence

J. Jenkins.

CHAPTER 48

A press conference was being held at the Town Hall in Birch Creek a few days after the wedding. Reggie and TJ had already flown to Ireland so they were unable to attend. They had written a statement to be read by Kendra who would be the main speaker at this "Her Voice" event. The Press conference was being held during the afternoon and the event would be that night at the High school auditorium.

Kendra grabbed the sides of the podium. A banner was hanging behind her that read "Her Voice." She was nervous, not about giving a speech but nervous for the other girls who would be telling their stories that evening in their voices. She adjusted the microphone. Cameras were flashing. She had not expected this big of a crowd, a lot of news media was present. This was a great opportunity for Kendra and the other girls to share their stories and get the word out.

"Good Afternoon," Kendra said to get the press conference started. The crowd became quiet.

"I was kidnapped, drugged and going to be sold for sex. I was able to fight back and get away from the man holding me captive thanks to a couple of brave men who heard me screaming. I will tell more of my story tonight along with other girls who were rescued from this torture. Unfortunately, there are others who weren't rescued or didn't have a hero step in to help them. Girls who still haven't been found, girls whose voices you'll never hear."

She took a deep breath, composing herself to keep going.

"We weren't lost. We were hidden, we were taken, we were sold. Some people looked the other way and some were a part of the network. This can't be a story you forget in a week. We need you to hear our voices."

The crowd applauded.

"Justice means nothing if we don't protect the next girl. We have to raise awareness and educate everyone on what can happen and how to stop it. "Her voice" is loud and getting stronger each day. Please come tonight and listen to us. Thank you!"

The crowd cheered and clapped. Reporters were immediately wanting statements from Kendra about her captivity. She told them to attend the event and hear all of their stories.

CHAPTER 49

"Breaking news: More arrests and missing girls found right here in the US." Nick watched as the banner floated along the bottom of the screen. He turned up the volume on the remote.

"Seven more girls were found in West Virginia living in a mansion used as a "Party Palace" for members of Rumsfeld Mason's network. Bidding for girls, sex parties, and a 'waiting station' were all taking place at this residence. Coincidentally, the house was owned by a well known congressman who had close ties to Mr. Mason. Other congressmen are being questioned with alleged memberships in this network.

Suddenly, Nick realizes some of the names he wrote in the notebook were known congressmen. He had no idea that when he heard Rum saying those names that they were politicians. He wrote those names down not knowing who they were. He kept remembering what the reporter asked him at the fundraiser in front of everyone: *"Were you aware that human trafficking was taking place at some of the events you organized?"*

Nick couldn't get that question out of his mind. He didn't know he was organizing events that were trafficking or bidding events. He couldn't sleep at night, thinking about how he organized the events without knowing what was really taking place. He kept listening to the news. He sat on his sofa, feeling numb to what he just heard. Then he heard a knock at his door. HIs heart dropped, who could that be? He peered through the peephole, it was Betty. Received he opened the door.

"Nick, you did what you said you wanted to do! You helped, you gave those names in that notebook and now these men are going to prison! And best of all, more girls were found because of you!" She hugged him.

"I just saw the news and can't believe what I was hearing. I guess I did help."

"Of course you did!" Betty grabbed his hand to sit beside her as she scrolled through the channels.

"It's on all the news channels. This is big!" She smiled.

CHAPTER 50

Kendra walked up onto the stage in her local High School Auditorium. The other victims were seated in metal chairs behind the podium. She glanced over at each one and gave a quick confident nod. Myra was seated beside Natalie as they had become very close from the ordeal they had endured together. The trauma had bonded them together forever. The other girls were from all over the United States. The audience was still finding their seats as it was a packed auditorium. News media crews were all seated in the front 2 rows.

As everyone got seated, the lights lowered in the room with a spotlight beaming on the stage. Kendra looked beautiful, confident and determined. She knew this was her chance to spread the word and create energy around the indecent practice of human trafficking.

"Good evening, thank you to everyone for joining us tonight in my hometown of Birch Creek. It was important for me to have this event here at my old alma mater and in my hometown. Why you might ask? Human trafficking can happen anywhere, in any small town, large city, across the ocean, in the local high school." She paused for a moment looking back at Myra and Natalie.

"I was given permission from my 2 closest friends to recognize them tonight as the other 2 girls who were taken from this very small town just like me. Myra and Natalie, do you mind standing up?" She said turning towards them and motioning for them to step forward.

"Myra was an honor student at this high school working her part-time job at a local Pizza parlor here in Birch Creek, the night she was taken. She left work and stopped at the convenience store to buy some gum and a drink before heading home. When she stepped out of the store walking to her car, that is when she was taken. A pillow case draped over her head, shoved into a truck and took up the gravel road up the mountain to a remote location. We now know that Rumsfeld Mason's home. After a couple of days, Natalie was walking to work early one morning to the same convenience store where Myra had been taken. Natalie was a clerk at this convenient store and walked the half mile to work most mornings from her apartment. On this particular morning, Natalie saw a truck coming towards her and knew something was off, she was taken the same way as Myra and to the same location. They were at this home until they were put on a private plane, blindfolded again and flown to a compound in the Bahamas where most of these other girls seated behind us were at too. The Bahama compound was one of the "waiting stations" that Rum Mason had all over the US and the world. These girls didn't realize they were waiting to be shipped via cargo ship to another country to be sold. All of these girls were rescued with the help of the FBI and Birch Creek's very own detective, Ms. Regina Memphis."

Kendra paused again for a moment motioning for Myra and Natalie to sit back down. She continued:

"Let me correct myself, Mrs. Regina Jenkins, she couldn't be here tonight because she is on her honeymoon. Regina, known as "Reggie" is our hometown hero who wasn't going to stop until she found us. With the help of a Chicago reporter, Terrence "TJ" Jenkins, who happens to be her husband now, is also a hero. He was the one who became interested in these stories and gave the nation the news about what was happening here. I was found unconscious in a hospital ICU unconscious after fighting my way out. A Brave Savannah Police officer came to my rescue and then my angel followed. My Angel was the ICU nurse who saw the press conference where our families were pleading for anyone to come forward with information about us. My mother and Aunt made a giant poster with my photo on it and that is how the ICU recognized me. He saw my tattoo on my arm and knew it was me. Reggie and TJ came to Savannah to identify me. I am so thankful for all of those who searched and rallied together to find all of us."

Everyone clapped and stood. AS they sat back down, Kendra continued:

"TJ and Reggie Jenkins could not be here tonight to be recognized and they wouldn't want the recognition to be focused on them as they are most humbled by the bravery of these girls. They have dedicated a new park to our town called 'Purple Majesty Park.' For those of you who live here, you know why that name is so fitting. This park is dedicated by them to the Birch Creek Community in honor of healing, hope and home. If you haven't seen it yet, please check it out." She paused and let the audience clap as a photo of the park sign flashed across the screen.

"Before I turn it over to our other guest speakers, I want all of you to know that to stand up here and tell a nightmare of a story is hard for all of these girls, they feel vulnerable once again but I know all of you will show your support. These girls were not lost, they didn't run away, they were all taken. I need everyone to listen to their stories so you can help educate America on what is happening and how to take precautions. I know today we had more breaking news that more girls were recovered and arrests are being made, this is a wonderful day in history! We can't continue to let human trafficking take place. For those who don't know, big sporting events that take place around the world and right here in the US is a big potential for human trafficking to take place. Men have been known to order who they want when they arrive in town and bid on other girls too. This is disgusting! I could go on and on but I will turn it over to our guests to tell their stories. Let's give a big welcome to all of these brave women!"

Each of the girls, one by one. Told how they were taken and what happened. They also talked about the girls who had not been rescued right away and what experiences they went through. They also mentioned girls they met who have not been found.

Kendra knew they could make a difference not just in this town but everywhere. She looked over smiling at her mother and her Aunt who were her biggest supporters.

CHAPTER 51
ONE MONTH LATER

Reggie and TJ were back at their penthouse in Chicago visiting his family after their lengthy honeymoon in Ireland. They would stay in Chicago for a few days before returning to their house in St. Simons. Reggie was anxious to know the latest on the FBI investigation. She stood barefoot in the kitchen holding her mug of coffee that she hadn't sipped yet. She stared out the window watching the city waking up below. TJ flipped through channels without a sound. News headlines scrolled across the bottom of the screen. More arrests, sealed indictments and more to come on the developing story. Reggie turned.

"Still nothing new reported?" she asked. "No names yet."

"I heard that Rum kept some files. I am surprised he would do that as calculating as he tried to be."

"Apparently, they are still sorting through all of it." Reggie heard her phone ringing in the bedroom and went to answer it.

After a minute or two, TJ walked into the bedroom hearing her talking to Sheriff Johnson on her cell phone. She started jumping up and down. He was going to get dressed to go out.

"Oh my goodness, that is awesome news!" She said, "How many did they find and where?" TJ couldn't hear the responses the sheriff was giving but it was obviously great news. When Reggie hung up, she ran over and hugged TJ.

"They found 15 more girls that had been sold into Rum's network. They are all safe and back home now. They were found in Taiwan."

"That is fantastic news. I know they will find even more now." TJ said with confidence. "Reggie, I don't think you realize the magnitude of this, if it wasn't for you, all of these girls would still be missing. I am so proud of you."

"It wasn't just me, others played a big part in this too."

"Now it's up to others, not you. Rum is dead and we are moving on." TJ got dressed. After checking his phone, he called for the driver to meet him downstairs.

"Reggie, I need to go visit the attorney to sign some papers, I will meet you at my parents house for dinner. We are going to plan that family vacation my father dreams about." He kissed her forehead and entered the elevator.

"That sounds perfect." She smiled watching the elevator door close."I was given permission from my 2 closest friends to recognize them tonight as the other 2 girls who were taken from this very small town just like

CHAPTER 52

TJ entered the downtown attorney's office. The security guard nodded, he knew Mr.

Jenkins. He moved down the hallway to the reception area.

"He is waiting in the conference room, this way." the assistant pointed down the hall. Inside sat Domino's attorney. Alone. He stood, smiled and they shook hands. TJ reached into his coat pocket and pulled out a thick envelope unmarked. He set it on the table in front of the attorney. Domino's attorney peeked in it, seeing the cash. It was enough to keep promises, and enough to buy silence.

"The trust is in place. Monthly disbursements begin next week."

"His story still holds."

"He kept his end, that covers mine." TJ said pointing to the envelope.

"He will be comfortable when he gets out." The attorney paused, then looked up at TJ who was already turning to leave. Then he said:

"The law doesn't protect the truth. It protects the story that holds."

TJ had no reaction, just nodded.

The deal was done.

AUTHOR'S NOTE

When I first stepped back into "The Link Series," to write "*The Weakest Link*," I thought I knew exactly where the story would go. But, as often happens with Reggie, TJ, and the people around them, the truth proved more complicated.

My readers were my inspiration. I was told by many that "*The Missing Link*," left them hanging on wanting to know what will happen next. I knew the story wasn't complete and my supporters confirmed it for me.

In the original release, I left the events of the night at Rum's house untold on purpose. I wanted you to imagine it for yourself. For this book club edition, I'm pulling back the curtain with a bonus chapter - "*The Missing Moment*" from a perspective you haven't fully heard before. It's the truth or at least one version of it, my version.

Thank you for taking this journey with me, for caring about these characters as much as I do, and for keeping the conversations alive long after the last page is turned.

JK Brogdon

MEET THE AUTHOR
JK BROGDON
Q&A

Q: Why did you decide to write a sequel to *The Missing Link*?

The first book left questions unanswered, and I wasn't ready to let go of the characters or Birch Creek. Also, my supporters told me that I had to write a sequel. I wanted to explore more of the characters in the sequel.

Q: The title, *The Weakest Link* suggests someone in the story is vulnerable. How did you play with that idea?

I intentionally kept it open to interpretation. Throughout the book, readers are led to suspect different characters. By the end, it's up to the reader to decide who, if anyone, truly was the weakest link.

Q: How did you approach writing the antagonist?

The antagonist is well known in both books. Rum is manipulative and careful, orchestrating events without getting involved. That made him more dangerous. He knows how to use people without leaving any fingerprints on the crime.

Q: Why did you originally leave the events at Rum's house off-page?

I wanted suspense and mystery of course! I felt that telling what happened would have given away how I wanted the story to end. I had it in my head but wasn't ready to reveal it. I wanted readers to develop their own version of what must have taken place on that night.

THE WEAKEST LINK BOOK CLUB EDITION
DISCUSSION QUESTIONS

1. Who did you suspect was the weakest link as you read the book? Did your opinion change?

2. How do you feel about Rum never being directly caught? Does this make him more or less threatening?

3. Domino's role in the story shifts over time. How do you feel about his decisions, especially at the end?

4. What do you think about the balance of romance and suspense in the story?

5. If you were in Nick's position, how would you have handled the pressure and suspicion around the wedding?

6. The bonus chapter reveals the truth about the night of Rum's murder. Did it match your original theory, or did it surprise you?

7. After reading the bonus chapter, do you see any characters in a different light?

THE MISSING MOMENT

BONUS CHAPTER

I heard a shot as I approached the front door, ready to enter the key code. I'd been outside long enough to hear the argument. Rum's voice, cold, calculating and loud. The other man's voice was calm, lower, and steady. When the arguing stopped, I started to enter hearing the shot ring out loudly. I drew my gun, walked in slowly, no sound but the smell of the gunshot. Then I saw him, gun in his hand, TJ

. I'd spent weeks following TJ and Reggie. I knew it was him right away. He'd never seen me, didn't know me, not until now. He turned towards me. A shocking look on his face.

"Who the hell are you?"

I looked down at Rum sprawled on the kitchen floor, blood soaking into the tile floor. He was dead. Then I turned back to TJ.

"I'm Domino."

TJ's expression changed, he recognized the name and started putting the pieces together.

"Are you here for him?" TJ asked.

"I was." I said.

There was a pause. His eyes turned towards the back door, then to me.

"You've been on the run from the FBI?" TJ still standing, holding the gun.

"Yes and hoping to find Rum before he found me. I guess you've taken care of that." Something shifted in TJ's demeanor. Still in shock but his mind was calculating what to do next.

"I need you to take the blame for this. You have a record. I will make it worth your while. I will retain the best attorney for you and give you money, enough to make you very comfortable." I tilted my head, looking at him. Here was TJ Jenkins standing over a dead body, Rum's body, bargaining with me as if this was a business meeting. The more I thought about it, it was a business arrangement. It could be a very lucrative business arrangement.

"Why me?" I asked.

"Because you have a record and you are here now. You know how to survive."

I thought about my odds. I have warrants, I know there are some who would be willing to turn me in. I'd been running on borrowed time. Finally, I nodded.

"Ok."

TJ extended his hand to shake mine. I held my hand up in a stop motion. I wasn't going to shake his hand with gun powder residue on it.

"I have to hear all the terms." I said.

TJ nodded yes.

"We have to clean up any fingerprints here and get the hell out." I grabbed a kitchen towel. After all surfaces were wiped clean and the scene ready, we turned to leave.

"I need to hear all the terms and details."

"Of course, we will communicate through the attorney."

I nodded yes. TJ left out the back door. I now was in possession of Rum's, TJ's and my gun. My life has just changed drastically.